THE ACCOLADE

C.M. CHARLES

ISBN 978-1-63630-763-3 (Paperback)
ISBN 978-1-63630-764-0 (Digital)

Copyright © 2020 C.M. Charles
All rights reserved
First Edition

All rights reserved. No part of this publication may be reproduced, distributed, or transmitted in any form or by any means, including photocopying, recording, or other electronic or mechanical methods without the prior written permission of the publisher. For permission requests, solicit the publisher via the address below.

Covenant Books, Inc.
11661 Hwy 707
Murrells Inlet, SC 29576
www.covenantbooks.com

I dedicate this book to the Lord and my husband Dave,
whose everlastingly gracious love and patience
has seen me through to success.

CHAPTER 1

The mother, who had grown up in a family of all sisters, had wanted five children of her own. Once grown, she married her teenage beau, and they soon began a family. First, the couple had two daughters, who were greatly loved by their parents. But in time, the parents tried for a third child. This time, it took a while before they conceived. Finally, when they did, the mother wished for a boy. Secretly, the father hoped for another girl because he knew to raise a boy in this modern age was quite tricky. All wished them well. One friend encouraged the young mother with "the third one's the charm!" She took heart in that, until one morning upon sitting up to get out of bed, there was a pop and water was released. The couple quickly traveled to the nearby hospital, after depositing the girls at their parent's home. The couple was amazed by the birth of a handsome baby boy. His mommy could hardly believe it was possible for her to have a boy, after having only sisters and daughters. The daddy was proud and pleased in spite of himself. The doctor handed him large shiny silver scissors to cut the umbilical cord. They had the child dedicated to the Lord as was their custom. They named him David.

Little David had an effervescent personality. His mommy was so proud of him, she could not stop celebrating his birth and calling him "boy baby." She made sure David wore all the adorable outfits kind friends had given her before he outgrew them. She nursed him for many months. All the usual raising took place, from teething to potty training, to learning to walk, talk, read, and learn all his subjects. David was learning to read before his third birthday. The most important thing had been to teach him about the love of God, who had sent his own son to die in the place of sinners.

However, when another baby girl came along, the boy grew a bit jealous, though he loved her dearly. His mother had less time for him, and eventually, his adjustment created behavioral issues. David did not grow out of it, as his mother had hoped. Instead, those issues continued and grew into rebellion until he began running away.

One day, when David and his friends had gone into the tall yellow summer grass of northern California to smoke pot, they were waylaid by a deadly drug tucked into the joint. David became unconscious. Later when he awoke, it appeared that he had slept all night and was waking up in the dew of the morning. His friends were gone. David, who was hungry for breakfast, rose up to get something to eat. Looking around, he saw a world he did not know. He began walking down a road he had never seen. It appeared for all the life of him that he was in some foreign country. In fact, it looked like medieval locations that still existed in European countries, on the travel series that he had watched on television. He saw crude signs along the way. They were in English. To the right of the road, David saw a beautiful manor nestled among trees and flowers. From where he stood, he could only see two gables and two tall chimneys. A tower rose up on the right side of the house. At the top, there were four corners that had blunt spires. In its center was a rounded roof. The tower had tiny windows. David thought to turn in, to see if those living there would feed him. But as he got closer, a man came out, shouting something at him. "David, son, where have you been?"

This man looked exactly like David's father.

"Your mother has been sick, worried about you. Breakfast is almost ready! We'll never make it to the festival in time if you don't hurry."

When David, who was quite dazed by the experience, came into the large house, he saw a plump woman who looked much like his mom. Younger children clamored about him asking for a lift up. But there was no time. After ingesting the creamy scrambled farm eggs and fat sausages with scrumptious biscuits and homemade jam, David rushed to join his "Dad" who was saddling up his horse.

David watched the procedure and followed it as best he could when saddling up the horse he was evidently expected to ride.

As they traversed down the country road, the horse David was on was jumpy with the realization that David was an inexperienced rider. The father slapped the backside of Maggie with his reins and David enjoyed a smoother ride after that.

"What is taking those pages so long to catch up?" demanded David's dad.

David gathered from the conversation his father was having with the pages and other servants when they did catch up that they were on the way to a place called Winchester. It was September and Father, who was a noble, was entered in one of the evening jousts.

"That must mean he is a knight!" surmised David with a new excitement that quickly turned to dismay when he realized his father might be killed.

"Will you be using a real lance today, Father?" queried David.

The two youngest pages, Gavin who was eleven and Patrick who was eight, laughed at David, saying, "Surely, you jest!"

But Father only looked at him with an odd curiosity. "Now, son, you know these are only games played with blunted instruments, don't worry the youngsters."

David was fearful of making another such blunder in his effort to become informed about the world he had entered into. Acquainting Father with this alternate universe was out of the question now. Surely, they would think David was out of his gourd.

And so, David quietly took in the countryside. It was green and plush, pastoral, dotted with sheep and other domestic livestock as well as wildlife. An occasional cottage with a thatched roof came into view. Small children played outside around its doors in the warm sunlight. He even saw a huge tree with its trunk made into a cottage, with a door and windows. The children, who inhabited it, were climbing it. The matron sat in the sunshine, which was gleaming off of the worn entry stone, her fat breast exposed as her newest offspring feasted delightfully on its nutrition. A man crossed the creek with a cart. Its wheels were quite large. It was pulled by one horse. He waved to their party as they strode down the road.

Suddenly, David saw a castle in the distance! Or was it a grand church? His father saw the awe in his eyes. "That's right, son, you haven't seen that since you were six years old… I'm so glad you are with me this time! Yes, as I have told you so many times this is where Arthur, king of the round table, ruled!"

David's eyes grew bigger, to take it all in. This was his father, but it was also another time. As they entered the city everyone seemed to know David's father, calling out, "There is Jack the Mighty!"

David overheard some of the muted conversations as other fathers recalled the incredible battles they had seen in which Jack the Mighty had pulverized the enemy.

"It was like David and Goliath all over again," one father testified.

His brother agreed, but clarified, "It wasn't as though Jack was small, no, not at all, but the enemy outnumbered us three to one!"

The first place Father led them was to the stable, where they could leave off their horses and cart. It had been hours since David had eaten, and he was smelling the wares of the fair. Thankfully, his father was too.

"Come on, my son," he said as he motioned to the youngsters who were also hungry. Little Gavin and Patrick wasted no time obeying. They had been orphaned at an early age and Jack had taken them in. He was like a father to them, and they obviously considered David as an older brother. They tugged at his hands, pulling him along. Turning his own torso upside down, David grabbed each boy around the waist with his strong arms. As he stood back up straight, the boys giggled loudly, finding themselves upside down with their legs dangling every which way. David again turned his torso toward the ground, sitting them down on stools by a table. He and Father examined the food choices and decided on turkey legs and corn on a stick. They gave the boys small tins of milk that were handed out by a milk maid. When everyone was satisfied, they rose up to explore the rest of the fair. Patrick stood on a chair, begging Father to let him ride on his shoulders. Father allowed him, but knew he must watch out for low overhangs.

"Now, we mustn't forget your mother," he said. "She asked me to look into some spices for her and some wool cloth for winter sewing. She asked me to look into Christmas gifts for our tenants also. Too bad, she couldn't come this year. She so loves the fair, but she is too far along to venture out. I will be on the lookout for new farm tools for myself. What are you lads interested in?"

Now that their tummies were full, the lads could see the rugs and dishes, household items, and handmade furniture. David heard many languages being spoken, so he realized merchants from all over the known world were there. This was so much more enthralling than the malls David was used to. And David's breath was taken away when they came to the Winchester Cathedral. He followed his father into the churchyard where they were warmly greeted by a churchman.

"This must be David! Why I haven't seen you since you were smaller than these lads," and he patted the youngsters on their heads. "Will you be staying long, Jack?" the clergyman asked Father.

"No, I'm afraid not. The little woman is expecting again and I can't leave her too long" came Father's answer.

"It appears you never do, Jack. How many is it for you now?" and the gregarious laughter of the priest was heard from afar.

"This will be our eighth blessing in surprise," Jack joined in the good-natured laughter. The younger set chuckled merrily along with them, though they weren't quite sure why. After a few more lighthearted exchanges, the four moved on to the pavilions.

Someone was shouting something about tournaments. Gavin and Patrick were jumping up and down with excitement. Apparently, Father had signed up for the first joust.

"Here's to King Richard!" David heard someone in the distance giving a toast to the monarch.

Alarmed, David wondered, "Where did Father go? Oh, he and the boys must have disappeared into one of those tents. They must be preparing for the joust!"

All at once, there was Father, who was sitting on his black stallion at the starting line. Shouts of "Jack the Mighty!" rose up from the crowd. David had never imagined his father like this, a hero! He knew his father was a tall man at six feet, four inches, but now he appeared legendary in his full suit of amour. There was a red cross over his chest and another larger cross on his shield. His helmet was tucked under his arm. Sunlight glinted on his fire-blue eyes which appeared lit from within and on the golden streaks of his thick curls that surrounded his head like a crown. His brow was broad and his jaw strong. Mother used to tell David, who was always big for his age, that he must not grow up to be "all brawn and no brain." David was certain that that could never be said of his dad. Father's opponent had been chosen to be a fair match, but was a bit younger. Father popped his helmet on and hoisted his lance as if it were a feather. Up came his shield, and with a robust swish, he was off. His opponent was on the ground in no time. The crowd clamored for more, but Father said, "No. I must needs go home, my wife needs me."

The disappointment in the crowd was palpable.

While David waited for Father, Gavin, and Patrick, he had a chance to glance around. Mesmerized by the charm of a girl about his own age, David's jaw dropped. She did not seem to see him, but her blue eyes danced with happiness. She was tall, for a girl. Her hair reached beyond her waist and was a thick sparkly blond. She was dressed in a deep royal blue dress with gold embroidered crosses around the edges. Soon it was clear that the other knight, who had come up against Father, was her brother, whom David heard her call "Silas."

All at once, Gavin and Patrick were pulling and pushing David along through the crowd to where David's father was. David lost sight of the girl. Desperately, he wondered if he would ever see her again.

"Come on, son, we need to get home before nightfall," called Father.

Once on the road, David took the opportunity to ask Father who the person was that he had fought with.

"Oh, that's Donald's son, you've heard me talk about Old Donald often enough. Remember? We fought in the Crusades together."

Flabbergasted by the revelation that he was looking at someone who had actually fought in the Crusades, David could hardly muster the courage to ask, "Who knighted you, Father?"

"You met him today in the churchyard, the priest. By the way, he christened you also!"

David no longer felt like an ordinary boy. He was the son of a knight! "Father…could I follow in your footsteps, could I become a knight?"

"Well, perhaps we can talk about you becoming an apprentice tomorrow, if the excitement has not worn off. It's a lot of toil and moil, my son."

The group reached home just as the stars were starting to twinkle. David could see the pride on Father's face as they worked together to put away the horses and gear. They entered the home respectfully, with quietness, knowing the others were asleep. A lit lantern had been left in the window for them. Father carried it along, lighting the way for the youngsters. Each found their bed. Father's feet could be heard padding their way down the long hall and up the stairs to his room with mother.

CHAPTER 2

※

David was gently shaken awake at daybreak. Father towered over him with a big smile.

"Ready, son, or have you forgotten the worthy request you made last night to be my squire?"

David was on his feet in no time, throwing fresh clothes on from a chest he found at the bottom of his bed. There was an armoire in his room, but he would explore its contents later. He only had time to catch a quick glance of himself in the mirror before leaving the room. He could not help noticing how good his color was. *I wonder if they brush their teeth here,* mused David. How could he ask them something he ought to know the answer to?

Father was standing over the stove this morning. "Your mother needs rest today, son. Love of God, country, family, and last but not least chivalry, are the most important principals to the knight. Besides, Mother made us a lovely cobbler yesterday, with berries your little sisters brought to her. She hardly opened her eyes when I kissed her this morning, except to tell me to shave!" With that, he gave a lighthearted chuckle.

Once they finished breakfast, they went to the barn. They would leave the girls to do the indoor work while they did the men's outdoor chores This did not include many of the chores done by the servants, whom Father evidently gave lodging to as well as a wage.

"Now, as you no doubt noted yesterday, a knight's warhorse is of immeasurable importance to him," Father instructed. David nodded. "You must become one with the animal," he carried on. "He raises you off the ground and carries you into battle, where you raise your lance which keeps you far away from your enemy. That is if you can connect it with the enemy's torso before he gets past it and comes after you!"

David saw this endeavor of knighthood as a rite of passage. *Perhaps that is what I was missing before.* But now was no time for quiet introspection. Father was bringing out the most beautiful young stallion David had ever seen. The horse was spirited, like David.

"I have saved him for you, Son!"

That moment was larger than life. Now this hands-on apprenticeship was the kind of instruction David could appreciate. He could not stand to sit for hours in school as the teacher droned on ad nauseam.

But as Father had promised, there was a great deal of "moil and toil" involved. David learned to saddle, ride, and care for the horse he had named Jasper. He must learn all about the armor a knight wore into battle. As a squire, it was his job to scrub, carry the armor, shield, and sword, as well as dress the knight in that armor. Father said Gavin and Patrick could continue to take care of his own war horse in place of David, who was making up for lost time. But David did take over for them when they were ill. David learned how to identify his family's coat of arms. Speaking of arms, David's arms were sore from strength training intended to enable him to raise his lance as effortlessly as Father had done. In the spring, there would be another tournament.

In due time, Mother went into labor and produced a beautiful baby girl. It was Christmas time and so she and Father named the little girl Noel Grace. Mother and baby needed lots of rest, which they got as everyone else took up the slack during her downtime. While the baby slept in the cradle, Mother wrapped the little gifts Father had brought back from the fair. David discovered that these were to be given out to the tenants who lived on Father's property. One evening as Father and Mother and the children sat around the hearth, they heard revelry in the distance. Before long, as the singing grew louder, it was obvious that whoever it was had stopped just outside the front door of the family home. The group of carolers sang loudly until Father opened the door amid laughter, and they poured into the large room where the family sat. They had a large bowl with some sort of spicy-smelling drink which they offered to the home's occupants. As they did so, Father carried a large basket with the gifts Mother had wrapped. He distributed the gifts among the revelers, who were the tenants on his property. Mother had also instructed some of her hired help to use her recipes for hand warmer pies and mini Yorkshire puddings. The Wassailers were happy with these treasures and wished all in the house good health before leaving. And good health was wished right back to them. David remembered going Christmas caroling with his scout troop, but the best they ever got at anyone's house was hot cocoa and cookies.

On Christmas Eve, the family dined on oyster stew with plenty of hot tasty bread and delicious shepherd's pie. David wondered what kind of meat was in the pie. He was told that it was "beaver, of course." The children laughed at him for teasing that he did not remember that they could not have land meats during the yule fast. They drank ginger ale. Everyone sat around the huge table. There was Mother and Father, Baby Noel Grace, Livia, Gavin, Patrick, Holly, Jane, Diane, Marjorie, Anna Bell, and of course David. Aunt Rebecca had come in from the village where she lived, to assist Mother with the food preparations and such. After dinner, she instructed Mother's hired help to clean up and they prepared for the next day.

Then Aunt Rebecca came in by the hearth to play her mandolin for everyone. They all sang concerning the birth of Christ. Father read from the Bible. The children listened intently to the story of when Mary was told that she would have a baby whose name would be Emanuel, which meant "God with us." Father read how Jesus would save His people from their sin and how Mary had gone to see her cousin Elizabeth, who was also pregnant with John the Baptist. She said her baby had leapt in her womb when Mary greeted her.

Father said, "When Jesus was born, there was a colossal star in the sky and it had directed the wise men from the East to come find the new king. The angels sang to the shepherds who were attending their sheep in the field."

The children listened with reverence and eyes as wide as saucers. David could not remember the last time he felt such devotion for the

Lord. It was as if he were hearing the story for the first time. And now the children kissed their parents and went to their beds as they were directed.

The next morning was one of the most wondrous celebrations David had known! A breakfast of hot tea and mince meat pies were given to the immediate family. Right away, David noticed that there was real meat along with the dried fruit and spices in his pie. That was not the way his mom prepared it in the century he had come from. But big preparations were already underway for elaborate goings on in the afternoon. The hired cooks who were in Mother's kitchen had already put a huge fat goose to roast. They were in the process of making bread and more pies with thick crusts, chock-ful of fruits. Butter and honey were already on the table. David could see that the yule fast was over.

Maybe it would be a good thing if we fasted before Christmas in the century I came from, he thought, *what with all the dieting the grown-ups do in January.*

Jack had made sure the vassals had plenty of victuals to prepare for the feast, and in they came with everything imaginable. There were delectable meats such as beef, bacon, hog, fowls, and hens. There were a bounty of vegetables cooked to tenderness, more fruit pies, and breads and cheese. David counted thirty-five people in the house, which included his family. So this feast would be shared like a potluck. The huge table with chairs for the adults and benches for kids around it could accommodate everyone. Father prayed the blessing over it all in Jesus name. That sounded so good to David, who could remember his Dad praying over meals many times. The food was delectable, and David ate to his heart's content. He knew this glorious celebration was for the sake of Christ's birth.

CHAPTER 3

⸘⸙

The New Year had begun with a burst of cold weather, which was conducive to fireside chats and stories in the evening. Some of the smaller children begged Father to tell about the Crusades again.

"Please, please, please!" they clamored.

So Father started in, "Well, after Jesus died in our place on the cross for the sins of the world, rose again from the dead, and ascended up into heaven to be with His Father, the Christian faith spread far and wide. But after several hundred years, a mythical religion was invented, whose adherents in time rose up to brutally take over the Holy Land as well as other land by force. When they were threatening to take still more territory, the state of affairs grew quite grim for its inhabitants. The status quo could no longer be tolerated by them. Finally, the Christians knew they must act. So began the Crusades in an effort to stop their enemies and to take back their land from the invaders. The conditions were grave. The enemy had taken hold in Jerusalem and had become unwilling even to allow pilgrimages to the holy places where Jesus had walked."

David spoke up, "Father, why were the Christians so easy to take over in the first place?"

"One reason might be because Christians are so peace loving and are willing to die for their faith if need be. Jesus told Peter that if he lived by the sword, he would die by the sword. Our first remedy to conflict should never be violence, if it can be helped. However, Jesus did allow Peter to bring one sword, presumably for self-defense. Also, a military or lawful protectors or police force may need to defend the innocents. Scripture tells us that in that case, soldiers don't bear the sword in vain. The Bible also says, 'And from the days of John the Baptist until now, the Kingdom of Heaven suffers violence, and the violent take it by force.' And so, we were confident in our mission to restore the land that had been wrongly seized, even if our blood must be shed in the process."

"Tell about the battle you were in, Father," David probed anxiously.

"I was in the battle at the first for Arsuf with King Richard the Lion Heart, in which the Sultan Saladin was soundly defeated!" came the jubilant cry.

"Did you win?" Gavin and Patrick chimed in, though they knew the answer.

"That we did, boys! But after that pivotal victory, Sultan Saladin took the offensive as King Richard moved us toward Jaffa. You see, our king, who would not risk his troops to faintness from the heat so prevalent in that part of the world, marched us in the early part of the day. He allowed us to refresh often where there was Adam's Ale."

"Adam's Ale, Father?" questioned David.

"Water, my son!"

The enlightened youngsters listened fervently.

"Our fleet was within spitting distance as they sailed down the coast to buttress the troops with replenishments and to give shelter to the injured. But there was a forested place we must pass through, better known to the enemy than to us."

"Did you meet King Richard" begged Patrick, followed by Gavin, "Were you a knight?"

"I was part of the mounted regiments of which there were twelve. Each regiment had one hundred knights. And yes, I was privileged to know and fight alongside Richard the Lion Heart. I have never seen anyone who deserved his nickname more nor fought harder for a greater cause. We knew that the invaders intended to continue conquering lands. So we must take the battle to them."

At this juncture, Mother sent the youngsters to bed, much to their dismay. However, Father continued night after night to tell his story by the hearth, during the ensuing winter months.

The next night began with a question from Holly.

"When did you meet Mother, Father?"

"I met your mother with her golden hair, rich blue eyes, and silky white skin when I was just a lad of nineteen. We promised our love to one another. But with war brewing in the Holy Land, I must needs defend our cause. And so at the age of twenty-one just after I had been knighted, I left. Never a man had a better cause to survive and return home than did I."

Diane and Holly exchanged knowing glances.

"Last night, you were talking about going through the dangerous forest," cut in Gavin and Patrick in unison. They appeared annoyed that the girls had, in their opinion, sidetracked Jack's story.

"Ah, yes," continued Jack. "The Wood of Arsuf is where Saladin tried to divide us in hopes of conquering us. Though the enemy outmanned us, King Richard, who was accomplished in warfare, looked out for the well-being of his men and our morale was kept high when he fought right alongside us. He was an exemplary swordsman, while no one could make a mark on him. We had English, Norman, French, Danes, Frisians, Genoese, Pisans, Turcopoles fighting with us. There were spearman and heavy cavalry. The Bedouin, Turkish, and Sudanese archers shot many an arrow, but our armor was sufficient to ward off much of it. Whereas, we were blessed to have skilled crossbowmen, who assailed both horse and rider in the enemy's army. The Sultan Saladin was accompanied by his own personal convoy and a host of kettle drummers, though he himself did not enter the battle! Saladin directed everything from below his banners. The enemy demonstrated their dependence on loud noise. Their war cries were unnerving, they blew trumpets, clanged cymbals, and struck their gongs. The princes and emirs of Mesopotamia, Egypt, and Syria had also sent squads into the fray.

"I, myself was honored to be part of King Richard's exclusive regiment of knighted horsemen.

"It was in early September. We slept one night, if we could, by a marsh on one side near a river. King Richard and we Crusaders came to be fully engulfed in the center of the Woods of Arsuf. In the wee hours of the morning, we saw Saladin's forces ready to attack.

Waylaid, King Richard would have us secure our ranks at all costs. But when the enemy attacked our rearguard, the knights must keep their shields and faces toward the enemy. This meant they must proceed walking backward as the crossbowmen loaded and fired."

"That must be what they mean when they say, 'I've got your back,'" surmised David.

"To be sure," continued Father. "Still we were in defense mode in order to tire the enemy out. King Richard would command the offensive against the enemy at the most opportune time. But driven beyond their ability to withstand, the corps of knights one after the other began to charge. Finally Saladin and his brother entered the conflict that their countrymen had begun in order to encourage his troops.

"King Richard was resolute in his objective of keeping the alliance together. But when he saw what had happened, he ordered the go ahead. If he had not, the men who broke ranks may have succumbed to the throngs of the enemy's superior forces. This was fortuitous as it caught the enemy off guard. And in the end, only several of Saladin's personal guards remained with a solitary drummer.

"It was indeed regrettable that the knights had not carried out Richard's orders. Perhaps, it is what had paved the way for some of our knights to go ahead of the rest. Verily, they were easy targets for the enemy. But Richard rallied the troops anew against Saladin, whose forces fled. Showing they had the spine to strike a third time, our adversary dispersed when charged upon and the battle was over, for the time being.

"In the night, the dead of the Ayyubid were relieved of the plunder they had no way of taking with them."

"To the victor go the spoils!" shouted Gavin and Patrick, taking David by complete surprise.

Father grew somber. "If only the knights had not broken ranks, we might not have had to fight again at Jaffa…"

CHAPTER 4

❦

On another night, the children entreated Father to recount the triumph at Jaffa.

"We went on to Jaffa securing it," he began. "From there, we yearned to make our way to Jerusalem itself, to capture it! King Richard and Saladin held unsuccessful negotiations.

"We spent Christmas in Latrun that year, then retreated back to the coast due to the foul weather. There we spent the winter months bolstering Ascalon, after having recaptured it. Bouts with the opposing armies went on simultaneously with the mediation of our leaders. But in the spring, we were spurred on toward Jerusalem. We were within sight of it! But once again, there was tension among our leaders."

"Why, Father why?" David heard himself protest.

"Well, son, that is a fine question. "Perhaps, when men are far away from their homes for a long time in a foreign country, it is hard to maintain cohesion. Also, the enemy has the tactical advantage of knowing the lay of the land and such. At any rate, news of Richard's brother reached him as well as that of the King of France, Phillip Augustus. Whatever the Lion Heart heard must have concerned him greatly, as he readied for a quick departure from the Holy Land.

"I will never forget the moment King Richard received news that Jaffa had already been taken over by enemy forces. The Citadel was all that remained in the allies hands. I was blessed to be one of the fifty-some knights the Lion heart enlisted to leave the safety of our ship and to take up the gauntlet with a sizable assemblage of Italian sailors, crossbowmen, and infantrymen. Richard vaulted into the sea, working his way back to the shore. He was irate upon seeing the Muslim banner in the hard-fought for territory.

"King Richard himself led the attack against the onslaught! Soon the enemy was on the run. But Saladin would not leave it there, especially after news that reinforcements were on the way.

"Once again, our foes were discovered hiding in the wee hours of the morning, ready to pounce. So our heroic ruler mobilized crossbowmen, knights, and the infantry. He commanded both knight and infantrymen to construct a hedge of spears and shields driven into the ground, which faced outward toward our adversary. In back of this barricade, the crossbowmen were poised, for one to shoot while the other loaded. The infantry drove tent pegs into the ground to impede horse and rider."

"Where were you, Father?" asked David.

"I was one of a small number of mounted knights King Richard held back in reserve. In my judgment, it was the crossbow above all else that won the day, most especially as Saladin's troops were made up wholly of cavalry. Their horses were no match for the bolts of the crossbow! And so, disheartened, wearied, and worn, our adversary departed in haste as several of we knights rushed them. King Richard himself headed up the spearmen.

"Genoese Marines may appear invincible at sea, but that is precisely where they retreated to when the Ayyubid entered Jaffa during the counterinsurgency. But Richard led the charge into Jaffa making short work of Saladin and his forces, who fled with their tail between their legs!" All at once Father's eyes grew distant. "I will never forget that day. King Richard rode along Saladin's line of soldiers, lance clenched in his fist. The Lion Heart glared at each one of them, as if to challenge them to come forward for a bout. No one dared. The Sultan was wroth. In the end, the combatants had lost several hundred men, whom they left to rot in the field and twice as many horses. Though we had a slew of injured men, only two crusaders had been killed. One religious man thought our enemy's judgment had come due, because of the many innocent lives that they had taken through the years, in order to force a counterfeit religion on the masses.

"A truce of three years was made between our rulers. Christians were no longer restricted from pilgrimages to Jerusalem. Because of the valiant Crusaders, the coast from Tyre to Jaffa was returned to Christian control."

"What happened after the crusade was over?" Gavin and Patrick wanted to know at the next fireside chat.

That night, everyone had crowded around the hearth. All day, the fog had been heavy, followed by torrential rain as the cold winter night set in.

"King Richard grew quit ill. But in time, he graciously offered me this land near Braintree, that I had greatly admired, along with its vassals. They helped me to build this abode, for Mother and me to raise the brood of young ones that were sure to follow!" The youngsters laughed at that. "This turned out to be a good omen as my father had remarried after my mother's passing."

"Did his new wife raise you as a lad, Father, was she nice to you?" wondered David.

"No, son, as I have told you, my mother passed shortly before I left for the Holy Land. I returned to find that my father had married a widow. He had given her grown children the home that I grew up in. He then had moved into her grand house with her young son. Her children's father had been quite well off, so the lad who had been greatly loved of his own father will receive much property and wealth when he comes of age. His mother's parent's being elderly have bequeathed all their property to him and his siblings.

"We would have been delighted to welcome Father's new wife and her family, but lamentably, it seemed as though she desired to divide and conquer my father's first family. Perhaps, she believed it to be the best way to control her own interests. At any rate, we've worked very hard to make a home for ourselves here at the Iron Bridge Farm. And we love attending church in the village of Braintree, don't we?"

Everyone nodded and smiled their agreement.

CHAPTER 5

As the sun caressed the earth once more, causing the days to increase in length, David was finishing the accelerated course on the obligations of a page. He found academics with a chaplain to be preferable to the boring classroom settings he was used to. He also relished the adventure of hunting with his father.

David was overawed with the Falconer, who used the amazing birds to hunt prey. And while he learned how knights must be assisted in battle as well as how to clean armor, pack gear, equestrianism, and chivalry, there were no expeditions or wars at that time. That meant that he could not put that part of his training into practice. Swordplay was fun to learn, but he was chomping at the bit to use real swords, not the wooden swords and spears he must learn with.

Finishing his training in hare-footed fashion, David entered the rite of passage as he became a squire. During a sacred ceremony, he swore on a sword consecrated by the bishop, prompting flashbacks from his time in scouts when he was younger. His lessons in the art of chivalry, most especially recalled etiquette he had studied then, such as taking off your hat or opening a door for a lady. But swearing on a sword was much more dramatic than anything he had encountered thus far.

Chivalry, a unique brand of decency affiliated with Christian knighthood, had as its time-honored code of ethics, gentility-nobility, or to treat others fairly. But it had as its most important component the sacred service of love and military duty. Indeed, the biblical virtues of faith, hope and charity, justice, strength, moderation, and loyalty were paramount for service as a knight. He must be courteous, exhibit fidelity to a liege lord, gallant during a justified conflict, and demonstrate military civility.

As a gift, Father gave David armor that fit, with a little room for him to grow into it!

Now David aspired in earnest to fulfill the requirements for his knighthood. That meant long days in which he must master the "seven points of agility." Father thought it best not to tell his beloved son, that once mastered, these all must be executed while wearing armor and that if David were to lose in a joust, he would lose both his armor and horse to the victor!

First, there was riding, which David had already made significant progress in, so he could participate in tournaments. David must be able to swim and dive, climb and shoot different types of weapons. He had been in wrestling in junior high and so that gave him a leg up there. But dancing! He had never been much good at dancing, let alone the medieval kind. Fencing, however, was what he looked forward to most of all. And then there was the long jump which he had some experience with also, from gym class.

During each session, David was enthralled with the connection he enjoyed with his father. They would share their hopes, ideas, and dreams with one another. Before he had come into this realm, he had decided that he had given his father and mother enough of his time. He had even told them he wanted to be emancipated and had begun running away much of the time, breaking his mother's heart. He made sure they understood that he did not want to go to school or church anymore and that it was not illegal to be a runaway.

"You can't choose your parents," he had mouthed off. Then he was free to waste his time smoking cigarettes and eventually marijuana. One night when he was a runaway, the police caught him with another friend, out after curfew. Bringing him home in the middle of the night, the police beat loudly on his parents' front door. His parents were aghast with their first thought of "something must have happened to David!" After the police left, Mother lectured, "When we were growing up, if we had behaved this way, we would have been kept at the juvenile hall for being incorrigible. And we would have had to go to a special school for kids who were truant or needed reforming. But these days the law does not back us parents up. Even when we turn you in as a runaway, they do little to help. You are free to run wild! If we were to beat you hard enough to stop you, if that were possible as big as you are, we might be thrown in jail."

"And if we chained you or locked you up to prevent your outrageous behavior, I guess we'd pay for that too!" Father interjected. "The police can lock you up for being unruly or breaking the law when it suits them. But if you vandalize or destroy property, who do you think would have to pay for it?"

It had been clear that Mom and Dad were beside themselves. In fact, David and his father had had a tussle once in which Father had broken his baby finger. He was too afraid to have it set because the doctor might ask how it had happened.

Mom and Dad had to learn what David already knew. When they had gone to a police workshop for parents with wayward children, they were given ideas to make the child's life uncomfortable or otherwise corral the child who misbehaved. At one point, Father had enrolled David in a workshop in which police connected with kids. David had enjoyed learning to ride a motorcycle. But when he got it in his craw that he was being babysat, his pride shunned the opportunity. In the end, the police admitted that if the child had learned to runaway, the parents were powerless to do anything about it. Consequently, David who often climbed into friends bedroom windows to sleep at night, was fast on his way to becoming a drug addict. "Good friends" had already begun introducing him to opioids. One of them mocked David's parents calling them "Jesus Freaks."

"God is a crutch," he told David, who was acquainted with such lingo. Now David remembered what Mom had said when she heard that saying. "A crutch is a dead, inanimate object, that we use to drag ourselves along. That said cigarettes and, illegal drugs, alcohol, or pornography as such are crutches. But the Lord is my Shepherd, I shall not want! He is alive! He makes me lie down in green pastures and so much more…"

Now David felt sorry for lying to people they knew at church and elsewhere about his parents. He had made them sound bad tempered and heartless. One kindly woman at church said, "Your mom? No way! Your mom is one of the nicest women I know."

Be that as it may, David who had continued to lie, to cover for his own bad actions was surprised at how many people he could fool. Not caring who he injured, he had told others, "I left because there was too much drama."

When Mom heard that, she told him, "And you're the one causing it!"

Finally, it got back to his parents that he was in self-pity, telling anyone who would listen, "I'm the black sheep of the family."

His father responded by saying, "All we want is for you to stay home, go to church and school like your sisters. When you are eighteen and don't live at home anymore, it's up to you."

David winced when he looked back on those events. More than ever, he was determined to turn over a new leaf. Those days seemed so far away now. At the moment, David was able to see what he had paid little attention to then. That was the elation in his father's eyes, when he had made his plans known, to teach David how to fix their old car that had stopped working. Dad had said, "My father owned a gas station when I was growing up. Sometimes, people would sell secondhand cars to him. Once he gave me an old Ford. We would put it up on the rack when it needed work. I thought it was time I taught you."

But David had no time for his father then. It was more fun to hang out smoking at the bowling alley. David realized a tear was trailing down his cheek, and he quickly wiped it away. He now believed that he had been given a second chance after coming here, and for that he was grateful.

But here, today the summer weather was pleasantly warm and they were headed toward the swimming hole. There, David would once again practice his water sports, including diving, which he was getting pretty good at.

"The most important thing to remember is to never, never dive head first into a body of water unless you have been in it right before diving," coached Father. "Things can move around so that if it were safe before, it might not be this time."

David was getting a swimmer's body on top of building up the muscles that were used to hoist the lance. His goal was to grow as big as Father and to at least give the appearance that the lance was as light as a feather.

David remembered how his dad used to throw him and his younger sister up in the air when he swam with them in the in ground pool in the backyard. His dad had seemed tireless then, yet he became full of pain and grief when David had rebelled.

"Poor Dad, I'll make it up to him now, though I wonder if I will ever wake up back in the century I was born in. Sometimes I hope not, but other times, I miss it. I wonder what happened to my friends. We really didn't know how to have real fun anymore. Our happiness depended on what we were smoking or ingesting."

David remembered the time that he drove a friend's car around the lake. He had not gotten his license yet, and while intoxicated, he had driven right into the lake. The passengers panicked as the vehicle began to sink, then they piled out and swam to shore. When David recounted his story at home later, Father said he had been concerned such a thing could happen and so had prayed for his son's safety. Before that, David had almost felt impervious to danger. Then a dark memory, of what had happened to one of the church kids he sometimes hung with, flashed across his thoughts. While at the lake on another day, that friend had been "throwing down" beers. So when the friend jumped into the lake and did not come up, fear struck in the hearts of the youngsters he was with. Once again, David had recounted the story at home.

"I remember how he looked up at me through the clear water, but he didn't come up. His eyes grew larger until I realized he was frozen. By the time we swam down to him, it was too late!" David cried, burying his face in his pillow.

This had been a cautionary tale that had changed the behavior of David's group. They could not even bear to go near the funeral or face the kid's parents, who were heartsick. But in time, the youngsters had returned to their destructive habits.

David and Father were on their way home with Gavin and Patrick, who wrestled like two cub bears in the tall grass. As they neared the house, they could smell the scrumptious supper Mother was cooking. Patrick was looking a bit sleepy already and had begged to ride on Father's shoulders as usual. But even he perked up, when he smelled the ham and navy beans wafting from the manor. The girls were rushing around the table with the finishing touches. Plates, napkins, and fluffy biscuits with steam rising from them and sculpted butter were just being placed on the table. A spirited exchange ensued about the day's activities, when it was noticed that Patrick had fallen asleep with his face in his plate. He never woke when Mother wiped his face and hands or when Father carried him to bed.

David was feeling rather bushed himself when there was a loud rapping at the front door. Father answered, hailing an old friend, whom he quickly brought in to say hello to everyone. David overheard the discourse of the two men after they moved to the great room. David knew that his grandfather was very old and quite ill by now. He knew that his father had gone to see Grandfather a number of times and had taken him on drives. But Father's friend, who had helped their family with legal matters, explained his concern. "I hate to tell you this, Jack, but some say this woman your father is married to, well, that her first husband died in an unclear manner. A faithful servant of your father's disclosed to me that he overheard her tell your father that she could cast him out of her house because he is so old and she said not in his right mind. She then imposed upon him, that he change his will. He must give up prime property that was promised to you, Jack. Give it up to her youngest son, as an inducement for not throwing your father out. Not long before that I talked to your father who knew me and asked about you and your family, so I knew he had his wits about him.

"Also, the servant's accusation rang true because of an earful I got when I was invited to camp at your family's creek. Your cousin and your father's wife were speaking in hushed tones by the bonfire, but I overheard enough to say with confidence that your father's wife has pushed your father into giving her youngest son the property that he had previously bequeathed to you. She told him you had your own property and that you didn't need his. Your cousin, who appeared complicit, said she would rather not have your family intruding on the property. After all they seldom come around and haven't improved the property. What's more, I can't stand religious zealots like them, she said. Your father's wife acquiesced wholeheartedly, stating that you had not paid taxes either. Naturally, I knew they were grasping at straws to validate their subterfuge, as you would have no reason to do so until you owned the property. Your cousin said she had a large family and she needed more property for her sons to grow fruit trees on and raise bovine. 'Tell you what,' your father's wife stated, 'I'll talk my husband into giving some out of the way property to Jack. We'll fix it in the will that Jack may only sell the property to relatives, unless none want it. Then you can set the price at the least amount conceivable. That way Jack can't whine about being left out and your sons can plant their fruit trees on the hillsides, and be well taken care of!' The ladies had a haughty laugh as they agreed that you were an uncouth son, who had not married well anyway, and that your children were completely lacking in the social graces. I would not tell you this hurtful news, Jack, if I didn't believe your father may be being maltreated and had I not been tasked with giving you this revised will."

Then Jack elucidated, "After my mother died and Father remarried, we felt even more unwelcome than my older cousin and her husband had previously made us feel. That is why we opted to stay away. As far as improving the property goes, as one of the older sons, I was privileged to be of an enormous help to my father, during my growing-up years. Father called me his right arm. But, I understood that because he had remarried, I must allow his loyalty to be for his new wife, who was not for me and who was especially antagonistic to my wife, whom I am loyal to."

David saw his father's grim face as he opened up the document. He read it at length. Looking up, Jack asked his trusted friend, "Will you be staying the night, Raymond?"

"I will if you want me to, Jack," he replied.

"Let's get your gear in and put your horses in the barn," insisted Father.

Next day, the men prepared to go see Jack's father. Raymond said David's grandfather had requested for David to come see him too. Lost in thought, David got his gear, but he did not want to see the woman Grandpa was married to.

"I don't think I would want anything from someone who spoke that way of my family, but no doubt Father knows Grandpa did not say any of those things himself."

Along the way, Father confessed that the only property he had ever wanted from the land that he had grown up on was the portion that was now given to the youngest son of his father's wife.

"I would have hoped to have at least been asked what portion I wanted, especially because I am blood related and from his first family, not to mention several years older than the lad," mused Father.

"It is stupefying, the level of covetousness I see in families when someone is dying," remarked Raymond.

Shaking his head in the affirmative, Father wondered why "those who already have so much are so greedy? My cousin's father and father in law left her family an abundance of property. And my father's wife had much property left to her family from her first husband and from her parents who had passed away, which she could give to her son. My father was very generous with her clan, as it was."

Raymond added some well-thought-out commentary, "I really hated to relay that whole quagmire to you, Jack, but I just couldn't see you caught up unawares."

David was reminded of the verse his mother often quoted, "The love of money is the root of all evil." But this did seem truly diabolical.

The group arrived at Grandfather's home in the late afternoon. They were met at the door by a portly, red-haired woman who appeared to be many years younger than Grandfather. Grandfather was lying in bed and barely awake. But when it was announced that his grandson David had arrived, Grandfather sat straight up and opened his eyes wide.

"You look just like your daddy did at your age!" he exclaimed and Grandfather pulled David in with a big bear hug. "Oh, and a little like your mommy." He smiled. David was heartened. But then Grandfather spoke in a quiet tone. "David, I had wanted to see you before I pass away… I want to see you in heaven! Have you received Jesus into your heart, do you believe?"

"Yes, Grandpa, I believe in Jesus," answered David.

"Have you received Him?" asked Grandpa a second time.

"I don't know, Grandpa."

"The word of God says that there is no other name under heaven given among men whereby we must be saved. In the book of John 1:12, it tells us that, 'as many as received Him, to them gave He power to become the sons of God. Even to them that believe on His name.' So it is a receive, believe, that is the power of God unto salvation. Would you like to pray with me, David, to make sure?" insisted Grandpa, who did not wait for the answer. "Pray with me now David!" Grandpa led David in prayer, "Dear Lord Jesus, I know you are God's only begotten Son. I know that you took my place when you died for the sins of the world. I receive what you did for me on the cross. I know you rose from the dead and ascended into heaven. I ask you to come into my heart."

As David finished repeating the prayer, Grandpa fell back exhausted, but with a visibly calm spirit. "Now, David, I am depending on you to impart this truth to your sisters, so I may see them in heaven also!"

David felt clean inside as tears rushed into his eyes. He would indeed impart this truth to his sisters.

David remembered that in his other-life Grandpa had been so strong. He would walk along with David on his shoulders on the warm sunny days, when he brought David to the park. Grandpa had said then, "'Behold the Lamb of God which taketh away the sin of the world'. Do you realize, David, it was not just good enough for our sins to be forgiven or covered, but they must be gone! That could only be done by the finished work of Christ on the cross. Scripture tells us that no sin shall enter into heaven."

David barely remembered his parents talking about their plight with Grandpa's second wife, after a grandmother David had never known passed away. He knew she was a very divisive matron, who had forced Grandpa to sell the home he had raised his children in or she would not marry him. The large sum of money from the sale of that home would be absorbed into his new family's finances.

"After all," she had said, her "home was much nicer." But she would leave it to her children in her will. Grandpa's land would be left to his kids she promised. But the woman was very cruel to David's mother. She had even cornered his dad, when he had his car up on the lift at Grandpa's gas station. While Dad was working on their family's car, the "old biddy" (Dad's choice of words) must have seen him as a captive audience. She began stabbing David's mom in the back, telling Dad that Mom should be out working. That was in spite of the fact that at that time Mom was caring for her two pre-school kids, one of which she had been nursing for eighteen months. Dad had said that he knew from that moment on "our family cannot be tied in with my father's new family." Afraid of what could be divulged about the incident when she noticed David's family pulling away, Grandpa's wife recast Father and Mother as reclusive and "goody, goody." She had even said their children were like "manikins." David's family could not understand how people could be so taken in, when his family were actually being shunned. Grandpa's wife had the gall to call Mother a "hermit." David wondered if his grandpa's wife acted with such impunity because she was so wealthy.

"Where my own mother was a uniter, that shrew is a firebrand, who is not satisfied to let us stay away in peace. She goes about smearing us while trying to make herself appear blameless," Father had denounced.

Mother simply quoted scripture as she often did, "Woe unto you when all men speak well of you…for so they did of the false prophets."

David was brought out of his haze of thought, when he heard himself being called for dinner. Being a boy, it took him no time to respond. He found everyone in the dining room getting ready to sit down. This room was elegant with high vaulted ceiling and an imposing dining table. David pulled the heavy chair out and sat down. As he did, he noticed the woman's son whom he had not yet seen. David judged himself to be six inches larger than the lad, that he had been told was a year older than himself. The rich delectable food turned in David's stomach as Grandpa's wife Millie blathered on ad nauseam. She told the worst stories about people her guests had never heard of and in gross detail. These were only punctuated by praise of Mortimer, her son, and of how well she had raised him in comparison to the way David's mom had raised her kids. Mortimer's nose was high in the air, as he looked down it at David. Only once did Millie ask what Father was training David for. But knowing the character of this woman, David rightly expected a barb. Sure enough, after hearing Father's answer, Millie clucked, "Other people's sons can save or die for the Kingdom for all I care, mine is destined to be among those who will rule it! I never wanted my son to be all brawn and no brains."

"Well, that is one thing David will never be accused of! He has more brains than his obvious brawn," came Father's boisterous laugh.

Undeterred, the vixen carried on imputing all manner of mischief to those she referred to as "hellions." However, Mortimer was clearly on a cloud of his own imagination, of what he would become…someday. Mommy would see to it. Mortimer knew that she had already secured for him the land that should have gone to Jack.

A feeble David came from Grandfather's direction. David ran to Grandfather's side.

"David, come here, son," the elder whispered into his grandson's ear as he lifted something from his own breast. It was a key that had been hidden in his clothing. "Quickly, put this chain around your neck! You must take this key to the abbey, where you will find a secret passage. When you climb the many stairs, you will find a large room. Look up high for a lion carved into the brace of the wall. It will be dipped in gold. Beneath it, there will be a keyhole, flush with the wall. When you turn the key, you will find another passage."

"Then, what will I find, Grandpa?"

"The way back…" declared the patriarch, and he fell on his pillow as though dead.

David had barely placed the key around his neck, when he espied Father at his side.

"We must leave now, son," he said.

Once on the road, they bid Raymond adieu. Jack gave him a hearty handshake and slap on the back. But before his horse was out of sight, Brett, Grandfather's servant came running. This prompted Raymond to high-tail it back to the party. Brett, had been taken in by Jack's father, who had cared for the lad and loved him like a grandson. Still a fledgling, Brett was crying uncontrollably and trying to get the words out.

"Your father has passed away, Jack!" was all he could muster until he sat down to rest. The clan offered him water and a blanket around his shoulders. "I wanted to speak to you before you left, Jack, but that woman sent me on a wild goose chase to try to find mushrooms for the meal she was having prepared. When I returned, you were gone and your father was growing cold in death. I announced the tragedy to the household. Mortimer immediately ran to your father's body and savagely ripped his clothing apart. He was livid when he could not find the key. I asked him, 'What key?' He just kept saying it, 'The key, the key…' His mother was wroth with me, supposing I had stolen it. I had almost convinced her I was innocent when she sent me to see if you had taken it, Jack."

"No, no" was Father's controlled reply, "I know nothing of a key. Do you know anything about a key, Raymond?"

"Not at all," rejoined Raymond.

"With bared teeth, she told me not to come back without it…" cried Brett.

"You need not go back at all. You may live with us from now on if you wish," Jack offered the young fledgling refuge.

Brett appeared greatly relieved, and Raymond agreed with Jack.

"Yes, the will gives you the decision as to where you would like to reside upon your master's death."

Raymond offered his sympathies, and after explaining he would try to make it back to the funeral in three days, he departed once more.

By the time they reached home, Brett had borne his soul to Jack and David, and Gavin had fallen asleep. Brett confided his grief over his master's last days. "I begged her to allow me to feed him more and to give him more to drink. But she would say that she did not want to prolong his misery by keeping him here longer than is humane."

"I also felt that something was wrong and most gingerly requested as much of her before I left," Father confessed. "But as I walked away, I heard her mutter under her breath, 'You should talk. You were never a good son. You didn't deserve the land my son got!'"

David listened to these histrionics as he never had listened to such goings-on in his former existence. Was it because he was growing up or because his head was finally cleared from the drug-induced fog he had lived in for too long. David could not understand the level of covetousness he witnessed. Father had told him, "People may be fearful of being left destitute in the event of someone's death."

But what about people who have much more than their fair share, who seek out a way to take some of the other fellow's portion? David was pretty sure that was what Mom had referred to as "ill-gotten gain."

It was nightfall when they reached home. Father helped Brett find one of the many spare rooms of the manor. David had been so caught up in the goings-on that the key around his neck had slipped his mind entirely. That is until he was getting undressed and the glint of it by candlelight drew his attention back to it! It seemed to burn into his chest just then. He must not take it off or let anyone know he had it, until he was able to fulfill Grandpa's instructions. David wondered, "Which abbey, and where?"

David, who could stay awake no longer, fell asleep pondering those questions.

Three days later, David and Father were on their way to Grandfather's funeral. They met up with Raymond along the way. After the initial salutations, their procession was thoughtful and devoid of commentary. Upon arriving, they fully expected to see the patriarch resting peacefully in a softly embellished coffin. They were surprised when no such sight awaited them. They were aghast to learn that Grandfather's remains had been cremated, rather than given a Christian burial. Jack would have seen to it that his father was buried next to his mother. *What kind of ogress does this to a man's first family?* thought Jack. But he already knew the answer. It was the kind that had no regard for others. And a verse popped into his consciousness. It was something about a foolish woman plucking down her house with her own hands.

Uncle Mitch, who was Father's oldest brother, had been chosen to give the eulogy. It was clear from the outset that he was using this opportunity for his own personal rant. He only elaborated on his father's ability to teach his sons to work hard. And he said that his father had not liked proud people. There was quite simply no endearment offered for Grandpa at all! David and Father were stunned by such an omission.

Afterward, folks gathered over a table of potluck brought in by family and friends. Raymond, who had much to attend to, had gone. Almost no one talked to David or his father after that. Each surmised that it must have had something to do with Father's urging Millie to better care for Grandfather's well-being. And perhaps because they had given Brett refuge. Both had seen this woman in action. So it was not at all remarkable that she would misrepresent them to others, which in her mind would be a fair reprisal. What bewildered them was that old family friends that had known Father for many years would buy it hook, line, and sinker, no questions asked. How would they not give the benefit of the doubt to their old friend? Didn't they realize Father had a side too? Were they positioning themselves to garner her good favor because of her substantial wealth? "The love of money is the root of all evil" Mother would quote.

Just before David and Father left, they were cornered by Father's cousin's husband. This was a man whom Jack had known for some decades since he had married into the family. Though the man had been left well propertied by his own father, he and his wife had a number of sons who needed land for their own families.

"Jack! David! I wanted to see you before you left. Sorry about your father, Jack, and your grandfather, David. I understand your father left some property to you, Jack. Perhaps we can get together soon to talk about what you believe a fair price for that little out of the way piece of property might be. You didn't want to come back here or you had no plans for it, did you, Jack? I mean, there will always be a place at the creek for you to camp with your family. Your father made sure of that in his will. And we hope to see you there."

"Perhaps we can speak about it another time, Neal," Jack extended grace to the meddler.

"Oh, that's right, it is a little soon to be discussing these details," confessed Neal, "but in the not too distant future, I hope."

With that, the men parted.

Silence attended the father and son as they wended their way home. But Jack could not stop his thoughts. He knew that his cousin's husband wanted to be liked by everyone, but saw him as moving his opportunism through his own wife. Neal would let her handle the trenchant warfare while he moved in for the payoff, all the time preferring to appear the big-hearted one. Jack still remembered how his own mother, when she was alive, spoke of the veracity of his cousin and her husband.

"Assuredly, they are two peas in a pod" she had declared. "They act like they own everything already."

Father and son's hearts cried out within their bosom as they remembered their patriarch. Now his body was gone!

"That sadistic, merciless wench! It's as if she tried to wipe out Grandpa's memory, Dad!" cried David when they were a safe distance from anyone.

"I know, son," Father validated David, patting him on his back with his large hand, "she is a battle-ax at that! We must pray for such people, God says. If she does not repent, scripture says, 'It is a fearful thing to fall into the hands of the living God.' But she can never remove your grandfather's memory from the earth. And in heaven, he is known, for his name is written in the lamb's book of life. Our hope is that we shall see him there!"

This did calm David, who looked back just in time to see Mortimer, who had been hiding in the shadows and was slipping away.

"He must have been listening and now he is going back to squawk to his mommy," concluded David.

Nonetheless, David pitied Mortimer whose logic was warped. When he told Father all about it, Father warned. "You start out feeling sorry for someone like that and you'll end up feeling sorry for yourself. But we must love, forgive, and pray for them. Christians are directed by the Lord to be wise as serpents, harmless as doves."

"But I can't be that good all the time, Dad," started David.

"No one can, son. That is why the Lord says, 'All have sinned and come short of the glory of God.' We are not compared to one another, but to God. We all fall short by that standard. God's word says no sin shall enter into heaven. That's why he sent Jesus as the Lamb of God, which taketh away the sin of the world. Our sin could not merely be forgiven, it must be entirely gone for us to enter heaven. Jesus was willing to suffer so much on our behalf. We rest entirely on His finished work on the cross. Knowing this truth gave me the wherewithal to unashamedly wear that cross in the crusades to protect the innocents, who were being persecuted for their Christian faith."

David was in awe of his father at that moment, and he remembered that in the other eon, and before he was born, his father had gone to the Middle East as a young man after 9/11. But David had never asked him about that. Even when his dad had tried to share those experiences, David was ashamed now to remember how he had shined it on.

The key burned in David's soul, but he was not ready to go back yet. He must learn more about his new faith in Jesus first.

The subsequent months blew past in a flash. David and Brett were becoming fast friends and often sparred or competed with each other on their preparations to earn their knighthood. One day as they rode along on their horses, they recited their chivalry precepts. David would call out one of them, such as "Fight bravely!" And Brett would answer in the same manner with "Courtesy!"

"Loyalty!" shouted David, to which Brett called out "Gentility." David's horse jumped as he exclaimed, "Let's do the virtues, faith!"

"Hope!"

"Charity!"

"Justice!"

"Strength!"

"Moderation!"

"Protect the weak!"
"Protect women!"
"Protect children!"
"Protect churches!"
"Treat others reasonably!"
"Nobility!"
"Religious duties!" yelled Brett, and his horse reared back as he sounded off.
"Love!"
"Military service!"

This game usually ended when one of the boys could not rejoin. But today they lost track of who was winning when they saw the quarry they had been hunting. The lime hound had found the prey, but the boys had almost scared it away with their boisterous dictums. The valet was shooing them with his hand and putting his finger to his lips, a look of shock on his face for their lack of horse sense. The boys were mortified; however, they soon bounced back. David pulled out his crossbow, which he was becoming quite proficient in. Taking careful aim, David shot another wolf that had been eating Father's livestock.

"That's the fifth one today!" he announced. "And I wish we had more daylight to continue."

But the party did not and they heard Jack's horn calling everyone back. Throwing the creature over the back of his horse, David remounted. Brett gave a hand up to the valet. When the valet was seated comfortably behind Brett, he handed the leash of the dog to David. David had been given the hound when it was a pup and named it himself. His father had taught him to be the dog's master.

"Come on, Godfrey, good boy, you brought another one down."

And David patted the dog's head, as he secured the end of its leash to his saddle. They bounded through the woods following the path that was growing dimmer.

By the time David and Brett got back to the rest of the party, the deer had already been field dressed or gutted, and the dogs were scrambling for the best scraps. Tomorrow would be another hard day, as they would be butchering the hart Father had been surprised by earlier in the day. Noting that the hart had the right amount of tines on his antlers, Jack could not resist pulling out his crossbow. They did not bring Gavin and Patrick on these hunts yet. The boys were too sensitive about the killing the beautiful creatures.

Jack had explained it to them. "Boys, I would never kill anything I would not use for good purpose. We eat the deer and make leather from its skin for shoes and the like. We always eat as much of it as we can. We even give away any extra to the poor. As far as the wolves go, they are killing our sheep and other creatures. We can't have that now, can we?"

David and Brett saw that the deer was hanging on a heavy branch by its feet. Tomorrow, it would be butchered and the wolves would be stripped of their pelts. David thought, *These wolves sure stink. There are so many pungent or even rancid smells I've had to get used to here, but I wouldn't trade what I've learned for anything.*

That night, Gavin and Patrick asked Jack if they could sleep on their cots in the kennel.

"Our room is cold these days and the kennel is so cozy," they said. "Well, that would be the only reason I would let you tonight. Those dogs are so tired that they will not need anyone to stop them from fighting among themselves, will they?"

And the boys shook their heads no.

After a huge breakfast, Jack, David, Brett, and Father's yeoman went to the barn where the large wrapped deer was hanging by its hind legs, a pool of blood beneath it. After unwrapping the enormous beast, they began by cutting the skin close to his hind hooves, then pulling it down as if it were a piece of clothing. They pulled it down the entire body and over its front legs until they reached the head, which they cut off. Throwing the skin with the head attached aside, they took little notice as the dogs devoured the head, which was their reward for a job well done. The calves of the front legs were given to Gavin and Patrick, who pulled the tendon to make the leg move back and forth. The hams were separated from the body first. Then the body was cut in two along the backbone. Each side had ribs and shoulder and other choice pieces. After diligently wrapping each section, they gave a portion to the yeoman and put some aside for the poor. Jack would begin a barbecue in the afternoon after the pelts were lifted off the wolves and their bodies discarded. Everyone in the hunt party was invited. They would bring pot luck, and there would be plenty of leftovers for all to take home. It would be a full day, and everyone would go to bed bushed but peaceful.

CHAPTER 6

~~~~~~~~~~~~~

David and Brett had been practicing with their wooden swords for days. Gavin and Patrick wielded their smaller wooden swords, doing their best to emulate the older boys. Their inspiration was the upcoming tournament. It was going to be held at the castle of the family whose son had jousted with Father and whose daughter would surely be present. David hoped to wow her by the mastery of his sparring with Brett as well as his skillful horsemanship. His heart beat quickly, hoping against hope to see her angelic face once more. David was afraid he would not be quite suitable for such a fair maiden.

"Oh Lord, please shed your grace on me that I might find favor with her and her family too," he prayed.

The men had been packing up and could hardly wait to hit the road. Father had said this was to be an opportunity for the boys to see how it is done. And so, early one morning, they lit out after a hearty breakfast, for as Mother always said, "The army marches on its stomach."

They met up with many other caravans along the way. They were a boisterous bunch the closer they got to the castle. Now they saw it, an amazing work of art it was. It rose up, surrounded on all sides with water. The only path into the large arch entrance was across a long bridge. David's heart rose with excitement! A real castle! There were square columns on each side of the arch that had windows in them. On top of the open roof were openings in the stone walls for men to position themselves, so they could take careful aim with their bows and arrows, if unwanted guests arrived. It appeared that there were passages from the square columns to the other cylindrical columns. Both columns had windows.

Once through the archway, David saw an eye-popping spectacle. He believed there must be thousands of participants as well as spectators on the castle grounds. Special effects in modern movies had never duplicated such a scene. There were jesters and suppliers of all myriad of food. Colorful tents with flags and coat of arms on them. Young squires were showing off their skills and bravado as older men coached them. Pages attended their masters dutifully. Not even sports of thousand years later could compare to the excitement and inclusiveness of such an event. If only David could show his friends from that era. Life here was too busy for the way they and David had wasted their time, and there was purpose here too. You didn't have to wait to be an adult before you got involved in your real future. For a brief moment of clarity, David wondered, "What happened to my friends?" But there was no more time for introspection.

Father had decided where to place their tent, so they quickly set it up and David proudly topped it with the family crest. Inside the tent, David, now eighteen, dawned his suit of armor with the help of Gavin and Patrick. As he did so, Father's words played over inside of David's head.

"First, son, the Lord tells us to put on the whole armor of God, so we may be able to fight against the wiles of the devil. Also, the devil is the accuser of the brethren says the Lord. We overcome him, the enemy of all Christians by the blood of the Lamb, our savior Jesus the Christ. We must gird our loins with truth! Jesus said that He is the way the Truth and the Life, and that no one comes to the Father, but by Him. So the first thing we put on as believers is Christ. Then, we put on the breastplate of righteousness."

"But, Father, you told me that God says there is none righteous, no, not one," David had countered.

"The Lord is not saying you stand in your own righteousness, but we are to seek first the Kingdom of God and His righteousness. Jesus took our sin on the cross, exchanging it with us for His robe of righteousness. When we put on that breastplate, the Lord tells us we are putting on Christ's righteousness. Next we are to shod our feet with the preparation of the Gospel of Peace. That reminds me of another passage that says 'how lovely on the mountains are the feet of them that bring good news. Above all we are to take up the Shield of faith, so we may quench the fiery darts of the wicked. We take the helmet of salvation and the sword of the Spirit, which is the Word of God."

David was ready now and he felt invincible! Patrick and Gavin each took a flap of one side of the tent entrance, raising it to allow the fully suited David to pass through. He stood before Father, who couldn't be prouder. They looked into each other's eyes. David was almost as tall as his father now.

"Hurry up, son, let's get over to the test site and see how well you do on the javelin throw."

David waited what seemed an interminable time for his turn. It looked to him as though there might be one young squire ahead of him in line that could outthrow him, but he would see. At last, it was his turn. David barely made out ahead of the other fellow he had had his eye on. He would wait to see if anyone else could best him. At the end, David won the event. The other fellow looked surprised when David gave him a fist bump. David wondered why.

Now that he was warmed up, he mounted his horse as Gavin gave the crossbow to David. Patrick held up a cup of water for David, who drank it nervously. Cantering to the next event, that he had practiced for all year, David waited in line. This event was comprised of galloping toward a target at full speed, then shooting at that target with the crossbow before reaching a line, after which the challenger may gallop away in any direction. On the starting line now, David raced away at full tilt, stopping just short of the first line, simultaneously shooting at the center of the target, then rushing on, David completed the course. At that moment, he spotted Silas, brother of the damsel he had fallen for. David was lost in thought, *Could she be watching him from a window somewhere?*

David wondered what her name was. Would she be fascinated with his strength or find another more captivating? David's motivation sky-rocketed. He must out do all other competitors! After he was pronounced the winner of the event, he galloped on to the jumps.

Gavin who was tasked with carrying the flag could not keep pace with David, but finally caught up just in time to see David bound over the second jump and head toward the highest jump. Gavin's heart stood still. David made it, and turning around with a flourish, he raised his hand to the crowd who were cheering. Thrilled, Gavin's heart started beating again. Once again, David was in first place. He reached down to grab Gavin's hand. Pulling him up, David swung the youngster behind him into the saddle.

"Let's try our hand at sword fighting," he called out over the roar of the crowd.

They trotted to that event where David dismounted with Gavin, who took the horse's reins. Father was catching up to the squire and his page, with Patrick riding on his shoulders. The swords were wooden or David would have lopped off the head of his opponent at one juncture. Be that as it may, David learned not to have mercy in a real duel, after his opponent quickly turned, and placed the tip his sword against David's chest, where his heart was beating. Father's admonition, "If you start out feeling sorry for them, you'll end up feeling sorry for yourself," came back to David.

David and party were starving. He began quoting an old nursery rhyme. "Simple Simon, met a pieman…"

Gavin and Patrick joined in as the clan came upon the wares or delectable meat pies.

"Best fast food I've ever tasted," asserted David.

"Fast food?" Patrick repeated curiously.

As they washed down their vitals with apple cider, they were joined by the minister from Braintree. He had come in with Brett and his own son, who had employed Brett ahead of the tournament. Most lamentably, Brett had acquired a severe sprained ankle while working for the minister's son. It was impossible for him to compete in the games that day. But he and the others rested for several minutes in the tent where David took off his helmet gloves and boots. The conversation turned to Mr. Moser, who was playfully referred to as old Mr. Dozer. The poor man had earned his nickname because he often fell asleep in church, in the front row no less.

"Oh, don't speak of him that way," countered the minister loyally. "I've been privileged to visit in the Moser home, with him, his wife, and their lovely children all around. The children sit quietly by the fireside listening to the adults speak. His wife always brings me a good hot cup of tea and crumpets that I know she must save back for just such an occasion. She reminds me of the woman in the book of Luke chapter 7. And I know Bob Moser works hard six days a week to keep a meager roof over their heads. Sunday is Bob's only day to rest, but it is my day to serve them. I'm blessed to minister to Bob and all the other working men and their families that give their offerings so freely. If they don't expect me to show up at their jobs on time and stay awake for an hour there, then I shouldn't expect them to do so at my job. I must be worthy of my calling and hire, as they are of theirs. I am honored that Bob chooses to spend Sunday with us. No one could rightly blame him for spending half the day in bed. No, Bob is as good a Christian as they come. Why? Because he never seeks charity, though he could, but believes the scripture that tells us that if someone does not provide for his own, he is worse than an infidel and has denied the faith. He and his wife don't have much but share what little they have including their offerings with the church. Remember what Jesus said about the widow's mite? The others had given out of their abundance, but she had given more than them, because she had given all she had."

This minister has a way of speaking that doesn't make me feel judged, but inspires me to have right thinking, David reasoned.

David recalled one evening in the other era he had come from, when he overheard his mom bemoaning with his dad.

"I just feel like I'm in culture shock," David heard her say, and he listened up. "When I was growing up, the church was like our extended family, especially because my dad's job required us to move so frequently. Our ministers understood that they were the ones who led by their example, that they were the ones who must measure up to their scriptural calling to be worthy of their hire. That seems lost today. They seem more like the ministers in Ezekiel chapter 34. They rule with cruelty, feeding themselves while scattering the flock, whom they do not go out after. So often I hear ministers use God's platform for their own personal rant."

Dad agreed, "Instead of lending grace to the hearer, such as scripture speaks of, all too often ministers use their unique opportunity to bloviate. No wonder the church is so disjointed at this moment in time. When I got saved, most of my friends and family turned on me in pretty short order. Scripture says, 'They think it strange that you don't run with them.' I really needed the church to be my spiritual family."

Mom came in, "I was so discouraged when David ran away that I called the hotline at the church for prayer. No one ever called back." Mom sighed.

"I know, when you first led me to Christ," Dad volleyed, "when we were teens, the minister was so good to us. He and his wife just lived in a little mobile home on the church's property, but he would invite me over for donut fondue. We would talk about the things of the Lord and pray. I learned a lot from him. He was such a humble man. When you and I were in high school, you told me our first date had to be to church." Dad laughed. "Those people, even men, acted like they really knew…loved God! It was only a matter of time before you led me to Christ."

"In those days, church was my best evangelistic tool. I knew I was accepted in the beloved. So I also knew anyone I brought would be treated graciously," Mom acknowledged. "I remember another time when I brought a girl from my school to a gym night our church sponsored. She was a foster care child being raised by wealthy atheists. She received Christ that night."

David remembered asking his mom, "Could it be that our church is too big?"

"When we've tried smaller churches, it just seems to give the minister an opportunity to bludgeon in a more personal way," she answered.

Then Dad opened up, "They lord over, making sure the flock knows they are not measuring up, without seeming to care about what we are going through or appreciating our worth! When we send an offering to a charitable ministry, at least they send us a letter of gratitude."

"Well, dear, how could our church do that when they never get to know us?" Mom lamented. "They throw small groups at us as though that were the answer. We didn't need that when I was growing up. Most often, there were opportunities for get-togethers where anyone of any age could come. There was never a shortage of aunts, uncles or grandparents."

"I remember it being that way also when I first became a Christian, and the ministers were always approachable and friendly," Dad interjected.

"Yes, and they were most often flanked by their wife who was always a gracious individual," joined Mom.

"Be that as it may, I've never seen those small groups ran well. Perhaps it is because the leaders are seldom pastors. They may be able to organize somewhat, but without a true leader, there is just a mishmash of attitudes, often petty among some in the group. The pastors seem to believe those groups absolve them from their accountability toward the flock. I gave up trying to go," Dad finished.

After a moment, David spoke up, "Dad?"

"What is it, David?"

"What is donut fondue?"

Laughing, Dad explained, "That minister melted chocolate in a small crockpot. Then we stuck cut up pieces of donuts with toothpicks. After that. we dipped them into the chocolate. Revved up by the Lord and chocolate, we'd talk half the night."

A loud call for those knights wishing to join the melee came forth. David's clan, having no one participating in the melee, nevertheless moved out of the tent to observe. A line-up of knights on horseback, on opposite sides of the field raised their lances and charged toward each other. Those remaining on their horses turned and charged again until there was only one knight remaining on horseback. Everyone celebrated the new champion whose name was Douglas. Silas's father came out to honor Douglas with a reward. At that very moment, David was struck with dread. What if the prize were his daughter, Silas's sister! Thankfully, the prize was a glittering sword greatly to be admired, though a mere trifle when weighed against her beauty. But where was she? When would David see her again?

All at once, Silas stood before David's clan.

"Ready for another joust, Jack?" he grinned.

Amused, Father fielded the question, "No, not I. But in a couple of years, you may find my son David to be a formidable foe!"

"Yes, I see he has grown into a stouthearted lad at that. We were overawed by your performance in the tournament this day, David. How old are you now?"

Wondering who "we" included, David answered, "I'm well over eighteen years, Silas."

"Hmm, my younger sister, whom you may have noticed is fast approaching her sixteenth birthday. She would like, I am sure for you to attend her birthday party. Shall I tell her you'll be there?"

Falling all over himself, David could hardly get the words out. "I surely would…when will it be?"

After informing David of the date, Silas elucidated on his father's efforts to secure Douglas in marriage to his daughter Lucinda. Once again David's heart sank. Silas went on about Douglas doing his best to entice Lucinda by kneeling before her and declaring his intention to go on a mission to the Holy Land on her behalf. He hoped that if he returned alive, she could find it in her heart to consent to be his bride. Of course, Lucinda would not give him an answer, but agreed to ponder his request. She knew "Douglas would be better for it in either case." Lucinda was also wise enough to know that Douglas himself may find someone else to marry before returning.

"She has seen such things happen before," concluded Silas.

So that was her name, Lucinda! It was a magical name, like music to his ears. David was ecstatic at the possibility that he may still have a chance to win Lucinda's heart.

The day of Lucinda's sixteenth birthday came. David and Brett set out for her father's castle. They each carried a gift they believed worthy of her. But they would have been at a loss without Mother's help. David having done extra work for Father had earned the needed revenue for the present which he had procured in the town of

Braintree. It was a golden music box which he had wrapped in lovely scarlet paper and tied with fuchsia-colored ribbon that he believed would adorn her hair in the most glorious fashion.

Brett carried a small box with a comb to fasten Lucinda's hair of gold. It was wrapped in royal blue paper. The young men made light banter on the way until Brett said to David in a confidential tone, "You love her, don't you?"

Startled, David answered the question with one of his own. "What are you driving at?"

"Oh, I saw your countenance lift and fall when Silas was expounding on Douglas's efforts to win Lucinda's heart," smiled Brett.

Exposed, David felt awkward.

"Sorry, I didn't mean to make a monkey of you," contended Brett. "I should be the one who is mortified at being so brash. I just thought we had some time to shoot the breeze and you might wanna toss the idea around."

"It's keen," returned David, knowing Brett was trustworthy. "Love with her would be a dream come true, but I don't know how I could be in the running against Douglas. He is more established than I and has already left on a crusade to prove his love for her," mused David.

"He is there and you are here. There is a theory, something about all being fair in love and…" returned Brett.

"Oh, yes, I've heard of that where I come from too," David beamed back.

Brett was just about to pry into what David meant when he said "where I come from," especially because it was not the first time he had heard David express himself so curiously. But just then, another young man came along, who was headed in the same direction. He introduced himself as Brandon and his younger sister as Abigail. David could see that the tables had been turned, so that it was Brett who was smitten this time. He would bask in his opportunity to razz Brett about it later, but for now, he politely introduced himself as did Brett. Because it was spring with all the blossoms on the trees and such, David thought it a perfect time for falling in love.

Once vetted by the jovial guards, who ushered the youngsters through the castle gates, the group followed the markers that were set for them to find the location of the party. They ventured through a rose garden replete with pink baby roses. They came to a door that was graced with a pink baby rose wreath and merrily guarded by a young servant, who opened the door for them into an enchanted pink room. Every color of Chinese lantern hovered over the celebration.

All at once, Lucinda floated into the room, taking everyone's breath away. Her very presence seemed to dynamize the room. She wore a pure pink satin floor-length frock with gold-flecked shoes peeking out from under. Ringlets and braids enveloped her head most gracefully, with pink satin ribbon bows intertwined among them. One two-inch wide barrel curl coming down her front side showed her hair to be waist length. As she moved daintily across the room to where David and his companions were clustered, she extended her hand first to David and then to the others introducing herself. In turn, they introduced themselves to her. Lucinda motioned to a smiling servant to bring her guests something to drink. When the opalescent goblets were distributed to the youngsters from the matching tray, David tasted of the nectarous concoction. He did not reckon he had ever partaken or a liquid he had enjoyed so much. But was it made sweeter by her presence? he wondered.

"Have you come far?" Lucinda wanted to know.

"Not too far," they all agreed in unison.

"Won't everyone follow me into the dining room?" called Lucinda.

The large number of youngsters followed her into a large room where a table was set with elegant rose-covered dishes and gold flatware. Pink candles and a crisp white table cloth embellished the table that was adorned with bouquets of pink baby roses.

"Won't you sit next to me, so we may be better acquainted?" offered Lucinda to David, Brett, Abigail, and Brandon.

As soon as they were seated, servants swiftly entered the room, placing several delectable dishes on the table. There were aged cheeses, cooked cabbage with ham, roast beef whose gravy boat was passed with it on the same plate. Gravy was to be poured in great quantities over the beef, potatoes, and Yorkshire pudding. Then came two servants on either side of a tray, like pall bearers, shouldering a lovely golden goose surrounded by nuts and pears! David, who was still growing and seldom full for long, was nearly moved to tears at the cuisine, but he dare not show it. Servants sliced the meats and helped each youngster with their desired portions. All around the table were boy, girl, boy, girl. The young ladies chatted vivaciously about weather, fashion, art, recent marriages, and babies that had been born, as the boys inhaled the sweet and savory fare. It was only when the young men were full that they joined in the conversation. So much so that the girls now had a chance to feast, for they were still growing also.

During this time, the young men did their best to impress the girls with their bravado, telling all about how far along they were in their quest for knighthood, who they had bested, and where they planned to have their next joust. Before too long, servants began to clear dishes from the table at warp speed. Then came the piece de resistance, the cake! Once again, servants brought it in on a large tray, candles already lit. Gasps of delight went up. Lucinda made a secret wish and blew out the candles. She cut the first piece and gave it to David, who was the guest to her right. The servants, going to the right of David, sliced, plated and delivered pieces of cake to each guest along with cups of hot tea, in nothing flat. As hostess, Lucinda received her piece last. The young guests luxuriated in the taste of the choice confection, chatting amicably until they heard the music being played by minstrels, in the garden. Lucinda rose from her seat, motioning for all to follow.

Once in the garden, the youngsters mingled with one another. Then Lucinda took the lead, gently taking hold of David's hand, who knew he should catch hold of another young lady's hand, who knew she should take hold of Brett's hand, who took hold of Abigail's hand and so on. In a short time, there was a line of boy, girl, boy, girl dancing to the melody. David marveled at Lucinda's soft hand. *It feels like a velvety cotton ball,* he thought. Then the line took on the shape of a circle. They danced to their hearts' content, until they fell into the benches giggling. After that, quiet conversations started up, as the music continued in rarefied form. Lucinda and David had ended up on a bench built for just two.

"You dance divinely" David told her.

"Thank you, so do you" came her demure response.

"Your hand is so soft," he told her, hoping he had not gone too far.

"And yours feels so strong," her reassuring reply emboldened David, who looked deeply into her eyes, saying, "Your eyes are mesmerizing and you are altogether ravishing. I hope you like my gift."

"What is it?" asked Lucinda.

"I want you to be surprised," returned David.

"Oh, please tell me what it is!" Lucinda begged.

David, who could not resist her, blurted out, "It's a music box, but I want you to at least be surprised by the tune it plays!"

"All right, I won't make you tell me that. I like to be surprised too," she added.

"Is it true, has Douglas asked for your hand?" David was embarrassed by his own boldness.

Stunned, Lucinda asked, "Who told you that?"

Beside himself, with his own daring to ask such a straightforward question, David answered, "Silas mentioned it after Douglas won the sword at the tournament."

"I have given Douglas no promise" she put it simply, "won't you call me Lucy…my closest friends do."

David was in a dream world at that moment, saying, "I would be honored to call you Lucy. You are most lovely."

Lucy blushed. "Thank you."

Desiring to make his intensions known, he appealed to her, "May I see you again?"

"We could meet at church" she suggested.

Spurred on, David agreed. "I go to church in Braintree, where do you go?"

"We worship in Coggeshall. Will you come and go with us?"

Eager, David wanted to say, "You bet I will!" Instead he controlled his enthusiasm slightly, saying, "I would be most proud to accompany you to the Lord's House."

David recalled the scripture that told him that as a Christian, his body was actually the temple of the Holy Spirit.

"But wait, there is a Market Day in Coggeshall on Saturday. Would you like to go with me to that?"

"I will see what my parents say," smiled Lucy.

The couple looked over at another bench not too far away, where Abigail and Brett sat, who appeared to be engrossed in conversation also. Standing up, David and Lucy realized they had never stopped holding hands after the dancing ended. So Lucy pulled David to her door and asked him to "please wait here while I ask my parents permission to go to Market Day with you next weekend." Before long Lucy bounced out again, "They said Silas could go with us on Market Day. May we meet you at the River Blackwater?"

David was elated, realizing he could not expect parents in medieval times to allow their daughter to go out unchaperoned. All David could say was "Awesome!"

Then came the call for Lucinda to open her presents, which were lovely and befitting of her age. The music stopped, clueing in the youngsters that the party was coming to an end. They all bid adieu and went their ways.

On the way home, the young men had plenty to talk about. David allowed Brett to go first.

"Abigail is a year and a half younger than I," he began. "We want to see each other again."

"Lucy and I feel the same way," David disclosed. "In fact, we are going to Market Day together, with her brother on Saturday."

"Oh, so it's Lucy now, is it?" chuckled Brett.

"You'll be calling Miss Abigail 'Abbey' soon enough, I dare say," laughed David.

The young men did not want to open up too much about their feelings just yet, so they turned to their second favorite subject, food.

"Wasn't that a good bit of beef today!" started Brett.

"You bet, and what about that golden goose?" sighed David.

"The mashed potatoes!"

"The Yorkshire pudding!"

"The nuts and pears!" volleyed the boys.

"I have never tasted such a luscious cake and so pleasing to the eye," completed David.

Both young men were quiet as they relived the experience, their mouths watering.

"Tomorrow it's back to the old grind stone," Brett broke the silence.

"You got that right!" agreed David.

CHAPTER 7

※

David had worked very hard all week to earn his wage.
"Now I can afford to treat Lucy in a way she is worthy of, when we go to Market Day," he told Brett.

"Will you pick me up some cheese and bread while you are there?" asked Brett.

"I suppose I can do that if you give me the funds," answered David.

David had had a nourishing breakfast, so he would not get too hungry too soon. Mother smoothed his hair and patted his shoulder.

"So you really like this young damsel?" she pried as mothers do.

"Unquestionably!" David was not hesitant.

"Well, that's good. You're getting about the right age for it," she conceded.

Once out the front door, David galloped away at warp speed, until he got to the river. Meeting up with Lucy and Silas, they all gave a warm greeting to one another. Then they trotted merrily toward the Market Day, where they met up with still more mutual acquaintances.

Ere long, Silas decided to amuse himself with some friends who were closer to his own age, so he waved at Lucy and David, indicating they may go their own way for now.

"Oh, I'm so thankful we are going to be by ourselves for a while," expressed Lucy.

"Me too!" David declared, "or else, how could I tell you how utterly gorgeous you are today?"

"I feel that way about you too!" Lucy revealed demurely, "Now, where shall we go first?"

"Over there! To the cobblers!"

And David whisked Lucy's tiny frame up as he grabbed her around her waist, nearly running with her, her feet barely touching the ground. But Lucy loved it. She thought it was the next best thing to having her knight in shining armor ride by and whisk her up, fairly placing her behind him on his white steed. The smell of leather was delicious and the work of the cobbler was meticulous. One young man was being fitted for a pair of high-top boots. David's had high tops also, but his were of a finer leather. There were delicate shoes made for ladies, as well as the wooden Patterns that would be attached to them to keep their skirts and shoes out of the mud or other undesirable elements. Lucy wore white shoes with a snowflake cutout pattern on top. There were scallops along the top edge and a strap. She had attached tall Patterns to the bottom of her shoes, which also helped elevate her a little closer to David's height.

"Where did you get those balletic little shoes?" queried David.

Lucy could not stop laughing as she answered, "These are a creation of our own Cordwainer, doesn't your family have one?"

"Yes, and…"

As the couple turned around they were confronted by a troubadour reciting poetry, which he must have believed the youngsters would appreciate. They did, and David tipped him generously.

"Let's go over there, to the cloth merchants' awning," suggested Lucy, and so they did. There were lovely linens and silks. There were handsome wool fabrics and colorful cotton cloth.

"Davy, don't you like that adorable silk handkerchief?" prodded Lucy.

"You shall have it, my dear," said he.

"Oh, I shall treasure it!" gushed Lucy.

David was transported by his new nickname of "Davy."

David took Lucy's hand gently as he led her to the baker's tent. He thought about the plastic that would cover the scrumptious breads and confections if he were back in the twenty-first century. But David had never been happier in that century.

"Let's buy these buns and go to the cheese and meat tents to choose fixings to stuff them with!" he coaxed Lucy, who was keen to the notion.

When they reached the butcher's tent, they saw ducks and pheasants along with other fowl hanging for the consumer's inspection. There were other meats, some of which were roasted so as to be eaten whenever the patron so desired. The pair chose a barbecued leg of lamb. They requested it to be sliced.

Then moving on to the dairy farm pavilion, the youngsters added delicious cheese that monks were offering to their stash. David did not forget to get Brett's hard cheese, which he thought tasted like cheddar, when given a sample. Everything was packed into an enclosed basket that David wore on his back. The couple found a tree to arrange their blanket under. David brought out the soft buns which he sliced open with his knife. He then spread the creamy cheese on the inside and placed the sliced lamb on top before closing the bun. Then he served it to Lucy. He very quickly repeated the process, and the couple bowed their heads in a prayer of thanksgiving before polishing off their bounty. Mum had packed a bottle of cider in David's pack which he gladly shared with Lucy. As they gulped down their drink, they were satisfied and rose up in pursuit of more festivity.

The couple found what they were looking for. They quickly joined the many youth who had taken up a ribbon around the May Pole. Davy and Lucy looked into each other's eyes each time they came around. He wished he could kiss her, but knew she had probably never been kissed in this primitive era. When the dance had come to an end and everyone was giggling, couples went off together arm in arm.

Just as Davy had finished buying flowers for Lucy, Silas reappeared, asking, "Have you both been enjoying yourselves?"

"We certainly have! Look at these beautiful flowers Davy bought me!" And Lucy shoved them in Silas's face, laughing as she did it.

Sneezing, Silas quipped, "All right, you little sauce box, it's time we get going home!"

Smiling, David said, "You two sound like me and one of my sisters. But I guess we better get home, if we know what's good for us. All good things must come to an end."

So the three reunited with their horses, which had been feasting on hay. They trotted off to the river, from whence they had commenced. On the way, Lucy asked "Will you be going to church tomorrow?"

"I always go, unless the ox is in the ditch" beamed David.

"Why not go with us" asked Lucy, her brother giving her a sideways glance that said she was being too forward.

But David, who did not see it, would not have agreed with Silas.

"I would be more than honored to attend church with you and your family," responded David honestly.

"I will have Father pick you up in the morning, so we may all ride together," finished Lucy.

After a quick nod from David, they bid one another farewell and departed.

CHAPTER 8

David was up at the first cock-a-doodle-doo of the rooster the next morning. He was putting on his Sunday best and ate the breakfast Mom had prepared while teasing his sisters in the usual fashion.

Just then, a carriage pulled up and David ran out to meet Lucy and her family. David remembered the old saying, "You have to salt the cow to get the calf." So he respectfully said, "Hello," to Lucy's parents and told them, "You are looking very well today. I truly appreciate you picking me up, thank you."

"David, my name is Mitchell. I knew your father when he was much younger that you are now. We were boys together. We rode horses all over hill and dale in the area where your grandfather owned property. We were set to go off to the Crusades together when I had a bad fall. The doctor thought I may have broken my hip. Your father had to leave without me. Long story short, by the time your father returned, I was married to Lucy's mum here and Silas had already been born. We were living on my wife's father's property at that time, but he suddenly grew ill and died. He left all that he had to my wife, his only child, as well as myself and our children. Fortunately, I was very good at math, so I have been able to manage everything very well for my dear father-in-law's posterity. It has made me generous also because so much was given to me though another had worked for it. But I love my wife dearly, and I protect that inheritance for her sake, so she and our children will never go without."

"My own father always speaks of you in glowing terms, but he has never filled me in on all of those details, sir," remarked David. "I know that he immediately married my mum upon his return from the foreign field. And that after they settled down, they soon started their family."

"Yes, and it was not so long ago that your father triumphed over our own son in a joust," added Lucy's mother, causing an unrestrained belly laugh among all present.

About this time, they were arriving at the church, for they had made good time. The men got cracking, jumping out, they sat a stool down so the ladies would have a place to step as they exited the coach. Mitchell put his arm around his delicate wife and headed toward the entrance.

The youngsters quickly took their seats next to Lucy's parents. The flock had served by working all week long, with only a small time off. Now, they were served, or fed as Jesus put it, by those who received their hire through the offerings of those in attendance. David took special interest in something the minister was saying.

"When I was a lad, I often went out with my uncle to care for his vast flocks of sheep near the sea. We rode horses through the hills as we tended his sheep. I decided, after a number of times in which we had to rescue those little rams, that sheep were pretty dumb. But when I told my uncle I thought so, he simply said, 'Sheep are only as dumb as their shepherds!' I never forgot that. As a servant to God's flock, an under shepherd if you will, I apply that logic to myself. I see Christ's attitude for those he served. He said, of all the Father had given Him, He had not lost one except the son of perdition. He had compassion of those he saw as sheep without a shepherd. He fed the hungry, healed the sick, and even washed the disciples' feet. My vocation is to be hospitable to God's children, many whom have suffered greatly in this often pitiless world. At least they may know they will be encouraged here and accepted in the beloved. Our savior condescended to men of low esteem. He washed their feet and died for their sins."

When the service was over, everyone moved out to the garden where there was a picnic that had been planned. Everyone shared the food they had brought, as they sat together at the large tables. Lucy and David sat together eating the sumptuous cuisine, which David pronounced "fit for a king!"

"And his queen," laughed Lucy.

Lucy wanted to know all about David's childhood. He told her as much as he could in a way that did not give away his secret. He wanted to know all about Lucy's childhood also.

"Well" she began, "Silas, my brother, is seven years older than me. He had a twin named Paul, who passed away at just a few days old. This broke my parents' hearts, though they were thankful for Silas who was always so big and healthy."

"Oh," interrupted David, "I saw the tiny heart-shaped gravestone with Paul's name on it in the garden at your home."

"Yes," continued Lucy. "My mummy and daddy say they are comforted by King David's words from the Bible, after he lost his child. The verse that says something like, he cannot come to me, I shall go to him."

"Faith is the substance of things hoped for, the evidence of things not seen," David quoted a Bible verse he had learned in Children's church.

Lucy appreciated Davy's heedfulness, "They were unable to have more children until I came along. They have blessed Silas and I immeasurably. One day, I overheard Father talking to Mother. He said, 'Lucy should be spoiled, but she's not,' which made me happy. I think it is because I gave my heart to Jesus at a very young age."

"You too?" David was gladdened as he shared his similar experience of when his grandfather prayed with him.

"That is magnificent!" voiced Lucy. "Your parents have a large family. And they are all girls except you," she smiled. "How is that for you?" she asked blithely.

"It is not too bad," David laughed. "The girls look up to me, I guess, especially when I bring home ribbons from the market for their hair. And I have Father, Gavin, Patrick, and Brett. So it's not an all-girl house. Besides, it helps me to practice honoring the weaker vessel."

Lucy became reflective, "Mummy and Father are glad to have Silas and I, but do not mind having no more children in such a cruel world. Mummy, poor soul, thought it better to have only two children, rather than a dozen, if you lost half of them to illness."

"Still, the Lord has been quite good to your family," deduced David.

"That He has!" Lucy brightened up.

Everyone cleaned up, visiting with each other until it was deemed a good time to be heading home.

David announced, "I must get home in time to do my chores."

Lucy's father was impressed with David's diligence.

David galloped home at full speed until he came to the brook, where he often stopped to allow Jasper a drink. This gave him a chance to think. As he did, he turned Lucy's words over in his head. He had not taken time to consider, that in this ancient era, there were no penicillin or antibiotics. He became aware that consequently, many people must die or be dreadfully ill.

That brought to mind one of David's favorite subjects from his school days, American history. The Revolutionary war, the War of 1812, the Civil War, even WWI, were fought without such medical aids. Previously, David had romanticized the olden days but not so much now. He knew that other countries had made colonies in America. "When our founders decided to become independent, they should have thrown out slavery along with the other corrosive customs that foreign countries had introduced." David believed that the Civil War might never have been fought if that had been done. Just to think, that more US citizens died in the Civil War than all the other wars that Americans have fought in, combined. Family trees were wiped out. There were many orphans and widows, not to mention those maimed for life. Many of the people who fought and died back then, never owned a slave. They detested slavery, as did President Lincoln who died for that cause in the end. There were abolitionists and free states and the Underground Railroad. All of America had certainly paid a high toll for the callous or even brutal actions of a group of wrong-thinking militants. But Mom used to say that women didn't obtain the right to vote for many years after the black man got it.

"I think that all told, women may have suffered most, throughout all of history," concluded David's meditation.

Mindful just then of the sun's position in the sky, David mounted Jasper and hastily galloped away.

CHAPTER 9

The days grew longer and David worked tirelessly during the week on his aspiration and training for knighthood.

Most Saturdays, David and Jasper would show up at Lucy's home, either in the morning to accompany her family to Market Day or in the afternoon just to sit in the garden with her. Occasionally, they were allowed to go horseback riding together. Lucy's white horse Suzie cantered well together with Jasper. As the couple trotted along, they discussed their likes and dislikes. David popped off Jasper to secure a bunch of fox gloves for this girl he now loved.

"Scripture says a young man's glory is his strength," proclaimed Lucy.

"It also says a woman's glory is her hair. Got that right," grinned David, to which Lucy blushed.

The couple began discussing what the perfect marriage would be. They both agreed that love came first. Lucy stated, "Father says that the Bible declares, he that loves not, knows not God, for God is love. He also told me, 'however a man treats you before he marries you, he will treat you worse after.'"

"True enough," agreed David. "The husband is supposed to love his wife as Christ loved the church. Jesus loved us enough to die for us. So I figure if a husband follows Christ's example of such selfless love, that husband will also do for his wife what Christ did for those of us who belong to His church. He provides for and protects us. He never leaves nor forsakes us, he is with us always, even unto the end. He is always understanding. Remember when the disciples couldn't stay awake in the garden of Gethsemane? Jesus wasn't mad at them. He said, 'the spirit is willing, but the flesh was weak.' And scripture tells men to honor women as the weaker vessel. That is where we get chivalry from."

"My father is always that way with my mum," shared Lucy. "He says he couldn't do without her."

"Yes, I've noticed how close they are, like my folks," returned David. "That is how I want to be when I marry."

"Me too," agreed Lucy.

David was on a roll now, "The Bible says Jesus came not to be served, but to serve. He healed people, fed people and even washed the disciples' feet. Likewise, a man who is thinking correctly when he marries a woman doesn't marry her to be his slave, but quite the opposite. That is what my dad told me once, when I was ignorant enough to spout off saying something I heard another kid say about his mom, that she wasn't pulling her weight. 'I guess she pulled her weight and then some when she was carrying you kids around inside of her, before you were born. And she nursed you all and carrying you on her hip, washed your diapers and a whole host of other deeds. She did all that before you ever lifted a finger to help her. And a lot of it, you probably don't remember!' I felt pretty small when my dad was done lecturing me." David laughed and Lucy laughed with him, saying, "That was pretty audacious of you!"

"Well, Jesus remembers our frame, we are but dust. That's what comforts me," finished David, in his usual self-effacing mode.

The young people's parents were watching the romance build and asked the usual questions. But a traveler who stopped in at the castle of Lucy's family one afternoon had been sent to relay the harrowing report of what had become of Douglas in his quest to win Lucy's hand. Douglas had been captured by the adversaries and was in their Madrasas. The assailants wanted ransom for him and they were working to indoctrinate him. Silas, a good friend of Douglas, was horrified by his plight. So Silas offered to go immediately to gain his friend's release. His father was aghast at the prospect.

"I must forbid you to go, son!" he declared.

"You are our only son," Mother said.

"I know, Mum, but if I don't go, who will?"

"They will take you, and then they will have two hostages," surmised Father.

"Not if I take a ransom," asserted Silas.

"How much are they asking for?" Mother wanted to know.

The dispatcher's communique, which David had overheard Lucy's father reading under his breath, said something about "tower pounds."

"Have Douglas's parents received this directive yet?" her father asked the messenger.

"Not yet, sir, I understood them to be personal friends of yours. It was thought that the news might come better from you. And now, I must away," said he as Silas accompanied him to the door.

David followed close behind them. Out in the bright daylight, the courier cut a dark figure, as he was dressed all in black mounting and riding away on a black stallion.

The men made haste as they saddled up to go see Douglas's family.

Lucy and her mum were earnestly alarmed for Douglas and Silas.

"It is times like these that I wonder if these crusades are worth it," theorized Mother.

"David believes we had no choice," began Lucy. "It was either finally take the fight to the enemy or expect them to continue to seize more territory, until they came for ours. Many believe we needed to take back what the marauders had robbed from Christendom. Mummy, the enemy has conquered and subjugated so many Christians. Our leaders had to act."

"I know, Lucy. And the love of money is the root of all evil. That is what ransom is all about."

The men came back with the news of Douglas's grief-stricken parents. Douglas's father, who was very wealthy, had given Silas a bag of gold to help him make the trip, as well as to secure Douglas's release.

"I would go myself, as I have done in past crusades, but just now my wife is quite ill and I'm afraid this news will set her back even further," he had uttered in near despair. "Still, I take some comfort in your going, Silas," and his voice broke.

David drew Lucy away from the others, saying, "I must go with Silas, Lucy."

"I knew you would," she sighed. "When will you be leaving?"

"Day after tomorrow, at daybreak. It will take us that long to get provisions and supplies together. I must go home now to break the news to Father."

And he kissed her hand before leaving. She could hear him galloping away at breakneck speed.

Father was in the barn with Gavin and Patrick.

"Father, we have received heartrending news from abroad," started David.

Jack began by dismissing the boys, who insisted they were old enough to hear anything. So Father said, "Go ahead, David, what is it?"

"Douglas has been kidnapped and held for ransom". Patrick shuddered, though he tried not show it. Even Gavin was aghast. "Silas and I are going to bring him back!"

Father looked into David's eyes, "Well, son, I never expected anything quite like this, but I believe in loving your neighbor as yourself. I'm certain you are up to the task set before you. I would not try to stop you from going," he did not further say, "though my heart aches."

"We will be leaving early, on the day after tomorrow," explained David.

Now, Father knew they hadn't a moment to lose. He offered David all his best gear, including his maps, so that David would be well outfitted for the long journey and would want for nothing.

Secretly, Father sent Brett to the abbey to speak to the vicar about David receiving an accolade. By the fireside, Father reminded David of his best advice, complete with the pitfalls of young men.

"You have completed all that it takes to become a knight, son, now that you are making this selfless act. Mother and I will have a prayer vigil for you. But you must go to bed now. Tomorrow will be a monumental day for us all."

THE ACCOLADE

Long after David had gone to bed, Brett returned with news from the vicar. "The vicar agrees that tomorrow is the day for David's accolade. I took the liberty of stopping by Lucy's family's home and requested them to witness the event if they were able. They said they wouldn't miss it!"

"That's wonderful, Brett! Thank you for going."

Mother fed Brett a special loaf of warm bread that had been buttered and beside it a container of honey and another one with jam.

It was summer and daybreak came early. Silas had invited David to stay the next night at his family's castle. By the time he got out to the barn, Father was there to meet him. There was a look of peace on his face that he said, "Could only have come from a night of prayer with your mum. You must take Gavin with you as your squire. I'm sure Silas will need his squire to come along also. Gavin has shown great promise. I would not send him if I had any misgivings at all."

Once all the supplies were packed into the wagon, David headed out for Lucy's castle. Before he left. however, Father disclosed his intention, "Your mother and I will see you at the abbey this afternoon David. We wish the vicar to bless you and Silas before you go."

David had thanked them affectionately.

David spent the morning making plans with Silas about which way they would go out and looking over the maps their father's had given to them.

After the servants fed the family a hearty lunch, David spent time with Lucy. They held hands in the garden. They walked over the bridge that spanned the tiny brook, holding hands.

"Lucy." David said as he looked into her eyes, "your beauty eclipses all others! I love you!"

Demurely. she returned his passion, "I adore you my love. You are magnificent in appearance as well as in character."

David lost himself as he fell down on both knees, "Marry me. Lucy?"

"I would be overjoyed and honored to be your bride," said she as tears welled up in her eyes.

"Then you will wait for me?" beseeched David.

"Everlastingly, my love, everlastingly" returned Lucy as she sank to her knees beside him.

He kissed her as they enveloped each other with their arms. After exchanging a few more sweet nothings, the couple arm in arm rejoined the others. They were deliriously happy.

David asked to speak to Lucy's father alone.

"Sir, Lucy and I hope to receive your blessing on our desire to wed, when I return from abroad."

"So Lucy desires this, you say?" her father asked.

"She does, sir," David entreated him.

"I have never denied my daughter anything she has truly wanted." Reaching out, placing his hand on David's shoulder he spoke, "You, David, will certainly have earned my blessing and her hand when you return. Now let us go to the abbey together to ask the vicar to pray for you and for Silas."

The servants brought the carriage around, and everyone piled in.

When they arrived at the abbey, David was a bit surprised to see not only his mum and dad, but Brett, Gavin, and Patrick, as well as a number of other parishioners he and Lucy knew. Why, Patrick had even combed his hair and he was wearing his Sunday go-to-meeting clothes. But in short order, David came to realize that his family and friends had come together to honor him as he was to be knighted at that time!

"David, before you go into harm's way and because of your altruistic bravery, I would ask you to kneel before me now, as I knight you," the vicar sermonized.

Taking David's own sword, the vicar tapped each shoulder as he officially dubbed David a knight.

This has to be the best day of my life, thought David. *My Lucy has consented to marry me and I have achieved my rite of passage into knighthood!*

Up before dawn the next morning, David, Gavin, Silas, and his squire McKenna ate a huge breakfast, set out for them by the servants. The men had little else to do considering the preparations and goodbyes they had wrapped up with the night before.

David softened as he recalled Lucy's loving eyes looking up at him by the fireside in the main room of the castle, after they had returned from the abbey.

"Did you know they were going to knight me?" he asked her.

"No," she fielded the question, "they even kept it a secret from me. And I could tell from the look on your face that you were taken by surprise as was I at my father announcing our intentions to wed."

The couple laughed endearingly.

"I am praying that we will be back within six months, though Silas believes that may be overly optimistic," David confessed.

"I don't agree with Silas! There is nothing too hard for the Lord," declared Lucy.

"I am so thankful to be engaged to a bright and regal young woman, whom I can trust to pray faithfully for me," asserted David.

"And I know of no man more noble than you, Davy, that you would risk your own life for someone you scarcely know. That is so like the parable Jesus told of the good Samaritan," stated Lucy. "You might say that that is what this conflict between these two religious orders is about. One is tyrannical, viewing others as prey, forcing them to convert or pay the price. They are like the thief who robbed and beat up the man, that the good Samaritan found and took care of. Our faith is in Jesus, who came to seek and to save that which was lost. 'For God so loved the world, that He gave His only begotten son, that whosoever believes in Him should not perish, but have everlasting life' (John 3:16). We compel them to come to the cross of Jesus, so that they will be healed, but we don't force them. We believe in whosoever will."

Lucy had stood on the first step before ascending the stairs that night. Turning around, her hair glimmering in the candlelight, she looked directly into David's adoring eyes.

"I will wait for you everlastingly," she had whispered before they kissed.

"And I will return to you, my true love," he had promised her.

David hastened with the others to leave. The sooner the better, so they could return. As the men galloped away, David looked back at the castle. He could just make out Lucy in the window with a candle in one hand. She waved with one hand and he waved with one hand, while holding the reins with the other. He breathed a prayer under his breath, "Lord, let no harm befall us and please bring us back together again, safely, in Jesus name."

CHAPTER 10

The men were headed toward the knights, who were stationed near the River Liffey. They would stay with the knights and sail by ship the next day, headed for Marseille. From there, they would proceed to the Holy Land. In a matter of a few weeks, they would arrive at their destination. The knights had an enormous bonfire that night. One told a story of a close fellow compatriot, who had lost an ear by the sword in one of the crusades.

"I wished I could be like Jesus and put your ear back on your head, I told him. But the dog ran away with it!" he said, after which a savvy roar of laughter went up. David could see how comic relief might be a comfort to men of war, but he pitied the poor soul who must try to cover the loss of an ear with his hair. Still and all that was better than losing one's life or not returning to your one and only true love, who might love you all the more for your sacrifice.

As David lay under the stars, by the fire that was now waning, he thought of Father and his bravery as well as the other knights of old that David had read about. King Arthur, Sir Galahad, Sir Lancelot and all the rest, both real and legendary flitted through his consciousness at that moment. Would he, David, be up to the task set before him? He was now as tall as Father and had done exceptionally well at the tournaments that he had entered, but would he back down when encountering the challenges of actual combat. Douglas had presented as a superior warrior, not because of the colorful feathers coming from his helmet and shiny shield, but because of his great skill. Yet David and the others were now going to rescue Douglas.

David awoke with a start! Men were rebuilding the fire from the night before. He jumped up with nothing but his braies on. He was thankful for the warmth of the fire as he pulled on his hose and ankle boots. Throwing on the rest of his clothing, David downed his breakfast quickly. Grabbing his gear, which was quite heavy with his mail armor, David and the others headed for the coast.

One of the servants had gone ahead of them the day before to purchase their passage on the great hulk. They would sail for the next few weeks to get to the Holy Land. This ancient travel was very far removed from the comfort David had known in the twenty-first century. The sails burst forth in the exhilarating coastal winds. Some men were already heaving over the side of the boat.

"This will be a rough journey for them if that continues," Silas empathized.

The sun peeked through the clouds and the blue sky increased, as flags unfurled, with the sea stretching out before them. David knew the Lord was with him and with Lucy. Each day, he would pray for a safe return to her arms. Summer was a good time to travel. They slept on the deck under the stars. They hit the doldrums only once, for a day or two. Two of the sailors almost broke out into a knife fight. The master of the crew stopped them, assigning extra work to them.

"Ye must not have enough to do," he yelled.

Gavin was showing initiative, but there were times when he was all over the vessel and David could hardly keep track of him.

"Now listen, fella, I didn't bring you along to be your babysitter. You are my squire. That means you must let me know where you are at all times," stated David, to which Gavin nodded a bit sheepishly.

Silas suggested Gavin and Mac (McKenna's nickname) see who could climb to the crow's nest fastest. The boys scrambled. It was almost a tie with Mac winning. They all engaged in games on the deck. They played everything from hide-and-seek to card games. Gavin had spied a pretty little raven-haired girl, whose mother had named her Crystal, because her eyes were crystal blue. But Crystal stayed close to her father's vest and would only look at Gavin when he was not looking at her, so his brown eyes could not meet hers.

"I guess I'm too young and don't have much to offer anyway," he confided in David one day.

"Don't feel too bad," encouraged David. "I was just about your age when I first set eyes on Lucy, but she didn't know I was alive, or at least that was what I thought then. Later, she told me she had noticed me also! You'll have a lot to offer in time, you'll see," causing Gavin to brighten up.

The ship came into port at Venice one bright sunny morn. David was thrilled and rarin' to go, as were the others. He remembered reading a children's book with his dad, about Marco Polo's adventures. He wanted to see the basilica and the gondolas. How he wished Lucy was with him then. But knowing the ship would depart for the middle east in a day or two, after taking on supplies and cargo, made him all the more eager to take in as much of the city as was possible before then. Gavin, with eyes as wide as saucers, followed as close to David's heels as he could. Silas and Mac had also agreed to stick together with David and Gavin. They were amazed at David's knowledge of Venice, especially because it was the first time for all of them to travel there. They must take a ride in gondola. The gondoliers were masterful in their manipulation of the water taxis. They wore puffy knickers or pantaloons that gathered around their knees. Long boots came up to their knees. The youngsters crossed the bridge David had seen in his book, and they finished in prayer at the basilica. They prayed for the journey, for God's blessing and protection, that the Lord would help them bring Douglas home to his family and that they would all return home safely.

That night, they offered a local a fair price for a room and they slept peacefully, with their window open. The moon shone in, and yes, the stars twinkled. Visions of Lucy floated through David's dreams, with Douglas showing up to challenge David in a joust for Lucinda's hand! David woke up in a cold sweat. It was the first time he had dreamt of what he secretly feared.

"Lord, deliver me from these fears. Please let Douglas understand and accept that Lucy and I are meant to be," he prayed.

Filled with peace, he faded back into slumber until the sun awakened him, shining directly into his face. Shoving his fellow compatriots in the shoulder to bring them to, David was the first to be dressed and waiting impatiently for the rest. The household that had kept them had prepared a breakfast of sausages and milk toast for the young voyagers, who stuffed themselves and gave thanks to the hosts. Their hosts thanked them in return, saying, "Come again."

As the young men boarded the ship that would take them the rest of the way, some of the aforementioned passengers were there, among a number of new ones.

When they were about halfway to their destination, the crew came upon a beleaguered vessel. Taking on the passengers that had survived what appeared to be a barbarous onslaught, the crew gave victuals and dry clothing to them. After a day and a half, one man had regained enough strength to bear witness to what had taken place.

"A band of pirates boarded our ship, making off with anything of value. But most heinous was the kidnapping of our angelic daughter. To her mother and I, this is a fate worse than death itself! In fact, I am afraid her mother will die of a broken heart if her pride and joy is not soon returned."

David knelt next to the mother and father of the girl.

"What is her name?" he asked.

"Her name is Grace. She is nineteen," they answered. Putting his hand on the father's shoulder, David motioned for the others to come near. Bowing their heads, they prayed for the safe return of the girl.

"Lord, we earnestly implore you to bring Grace unharmed, back to her parents with all due speed. Please calm her parent's hearts with your peace, that passes all understanding. In Jesus's name, we pray this, Amen!"

Grace's parents described her appearance to the men and asked them to help locate her. They agreed to do so after finding out where to bring her if found.

Finally, the vessel reached land. The men set about asking questions of the residents concerning Douglas and Grace. Interestingly, they met up with a group who claimed to know of the whereabouts of both Grace and Douglas. They were also informed that there would certainly be a ransom involved, especially for the young girl, whom the kidnappers had hoped to sell for marriage to a wealthy sultan. Two of those men agreed to escort David and Silas to the location where they believed Grace and Douglas to be, for a price. David and Silas spoke privately with one another.

"I think it sounds fishy," David expressed.

"It's chancy, if you ask me," agreed Silas, "but what else do we have to go on? We know where Grace's parents are staying, and they said they could pay any price to have her back."

Reluctantly, the knights and their squires consented to go along. But Gavin said, "I think the whole thing sounds shady."

"It's far-fetched if you ask me, but what do I know?" asked Mac.

They must first procure camels for the group, as well as provisions. They would start out at dawn the next morning.

Now that they had made their decision, the bevy of young men embarked upon their quest. Such a trip was rough going, but they had adequate meals and rested well. Their guides knew where the best watering holes were, for man and beast. In due time, they reached a narrow passage whose soft stone was brightly colored in shades of golden amber. At the end of that passage, they arrived in an open expanse. David and the others were amazed at the architecture that was carved right into the mountain.

"It looks like something you'd see in a fancy ancient city, columns and everything!" exclaimed David. Then he remembered a documentary he had seen about this place. It was called Petra.

"I didn't know this place went this far back…" he mused.

The scouts led them into an obscure passage, where there were rooms filled with people. David's party was told that one room was for kidnapped future brides and another was for ordinary slave girls. They were shown a room with kidnapped slave boys and another with young men, who were being forcefully conscripted into a foreign military. Douglas was in that group! They brought him out into the light of day, where he fell on the neck of his rescuers.

"Thank God, my prayers have been answered!" Douglas cried.

"We have also come for a girl, whose name is Grace," David said.

"Does she have long red curls and green eyes that appear to be lit from within?" asked Douglas.

"According to her parents, she does," answered Silas.

"I've seen her when they bring out the girls for fresh air. They don't allow them in the direct sun because they want their skin as light as possible."

So Douglas accompanied the scouts into the passage, where the young ladies were kept, in order to identify Grace. Soon she was brought forward.

"We are here on behalf of your parents," explained Silas.

"Oh, thank goodness they are still alive… I wasn't sure if they would make it or…if I had anyone to go home to!" And she burst into tears.

Silas must now pay up to bring the captives out again. Grace's parents had given a tidy sum for her return, and of course, Douglas's parents had done so also. Once the boorish transaction had taken place, the young people were free to go with their liberators, back through the tiny passage. It was clear that there was chemistry between Silas and Grace. And by the time they returned her to her parents, who were full of gratitude, Grace was already referring to him as her knight in shining armor.

"We are indebted to you, Silas, and you may court our daughter when we get back to Ireland, if she so chooses."

"If she so chooses!" laughed Grace. "You know I do, Father."

As for Douglas, he had decided to stay and join the Knights Templar. He wrote his parents a letter, asking Silas to deliver it to them.

David missed Lucinda more than ever, when he watched Silas and Grace making over each other on board the ship. They returned first to Venice and then to Ireland. How glad David was to see its shores anew.

He rode like the dickens to get back to Lucy! But his horse stopped without warning in front of the abbey. It would not move. All at once, David knew what he must do. Grandfather had told him. David sent Gavin on ahead.

"Let them know I've stopped at the abbey for a bit," he said.

THE ACCOLADE

Gavin waved as he turned and flew down the hill on his horse.

Slipping quietly into the main sanctuary, David was almost surprised to find it empty. He leaned on a low banister which opened up a secret passage. He climbed the steep stairs he found inside until he entered a large hall. *This must be the place Grandpa was talking about.* The great hall he came into housed many artifacts. David began looking for the carved lion dipped in gold. He found it up high. There was the keyhole, flush with the wall! The key, almost forgotten, now burned into David's chest. Placing it into the key hole and summoning all his courage, David turned the key and found a passage inside the door, which the key had opened. Yet another set of steep stairs were there. The passage seemed to get darker and tighter the higher he got, until he seemed to be clawing his way through earth itself. The smell was earth, dirt. Bible verses flashed through his mind: "The value of a man does not consist in the abundance of things that he possesses… There is no other name under heaven, given among men, whereby we must be saved…whoever calls on the name of the Lord will be saved… All we like sheep have gone astray, and turned everyone to his own way, and the Lord has laid on him the iniquity of us all." A thought of what Mom used to say, "It's always darkest before the dawn…" came to mind. As he was clawing into the dirt in the pitch blackness, he broke into a dimly lit room, where he saw himself lying in a bed. He saw his mother on her knees, praying next to that bed. David was back in his body, and he could hear his mother praying for his life!

"Please, Lord, don't let them pull the plug. We've hung on these five long years, don't let the court take David's life from us!" she pleaded.

David was shocked! Had he been away for five years? His mind raced back to where he first lost consciousness of this space in time.

"Mom, I'm here!" he cried.

"David, David! Oh, thank the Lord you are saved!"

She explained about everything all at once, as she called Dad on her cell phone. When she was done, David understood that five years before he had gone missing, when a family pet found him in the hills where he and his friends had been. He was dehydrated, near death, and in a coma. It was believed that he had brain damage, but was not brain dead. All this time, they had been praying for a miracle. They were there almost every day, reading and talking to him. David's eyes fell on the nightstand beside his bed. Books like *Pilgrim's Progress*, *Narnia*, *Robin Hood*, and *King Arthur of the Round Table* were piled high on it.

"The pastor came to pray for you each week," recounted Mom.

"My friends, my friends," shouted David, "what about my friends?"

"I wanted to wait to talk to you about that when you got better," said Father as he entered the room.

David knew no good news would start out like that.

"What happened, Dad?" asked David earnestly.

Putting his hand on David's head, Dad said, "They didn't make it, son."

Tears sprang into David's eyes.

"I was such a rotten testimony… I followed…when I should have led," repented David.

"Well, at least you brought them to church when you were all younger. I remember seeing at least one of them go forward when the minister gave an altar call," Dad comforted, cradling David in his arms.

"You think they might have come to know the love of Jesus before they passed?" gulped David, his eyes searched his parents' faces.

"That is very possible. Think of the thief on the cross," Mom continued. "Many people who knew him may not have been there when he was dying. They might never have guessed that he, of all people, met Jesus in the last moments of his life! Scripture says that no one comes to know the Lord unless the Holy Spirit draws them, and that this is the light that lights everyone that comes into the world."

"Mom, I've heard it said that we will see people in heaven, whom we did not expect to be there, and some we thought would be there, won't be…"

"That reminds me David, Grandpa passed away while you were in the coma. He came to see you every day until he couldn't. He was praying for you to find the way back."

David would expound on the relevance of that later.

"Now, that brings to my mind the parable Jesus told, of the man who said to himself, 'Soul, you have much goods.' Then he tore down his barn and built a bigger one. But God said, 'You fool, this night shall your soul be required of you. Then whose shall those things be, which you have provided?'" David pontificated.

"Our son went away as a wayward adolescent. But he has returned, a man!" declared Dad.

At that moment, a flash of golden blond hair was seen in the hallway, but just for a moment.

"Who was that?" asked David.

"That's one of the girls who have helped with your care. Sometimes, when Dad was at work and I had dozed off for a bit, she would read to you. She's a Christian and new at our church" Mom fielded the question, not wanting to share the moment with anyone else, just yet.

"I'd like to meet her," smiled David. "What's her name?"

"Her name tag says Lucinda," returned Dad, "but I hear everyone she knows calls her Cindy."

ABOUT THE AUTHOR

The author received her first encouragement to write, while living in Biloxi, Mississippi. It came from Mrs. Fowler, her fourth grade school teacher, who had returned an assignment to C. M. with the words, "I expect to read your book someday." The author never forgot, but after getting married and starting a family early in life, writing was often on the back burner.

When her fourth child left home, C. M. began writing again. Only this time, due to many of life's experiences and a great deal of heartache, she had more wisdom and a lot more to say.

Lightning Source UK Ltd.
Milton Keynes UK
UKHW010626020721
386516UK00001B/39